CRYSTAL-CLEAR
DREAMS

Also by Marilyn Prather
in Large Print:

A Certain Enchantment
A Deadly Reunion
A Light in the Darkness
The Mysterious Merry-Go-Round

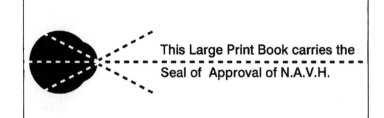

Crystal-Clear Dreams

Marilyn Prather

Thorndike Press • Waterville, Maine

Published in 2005 by arrangement with Marilyn Prather.

Thorndike Press® Large Print Candlelight.

The tree indicium is a trademark of Thorndike Press.

The text of this Large Print edition is unabridged.
Other aspects of the book may vary from the original edition.

Set in 16 pt. Plantin by Liana M. Walker.

Printed in the United States on permanent paper.

Library of Congress Cataloging-in-Publication Data

Prather, Marilyn.
    Crystal-clear dreams / by Marilyn Prather.
       p. cm. — (Thorndike Press large print Candlelight)
    ISBN 0-7862-8137-5 (lg. print : hc : alk. paper)
    1. Figure skaters — Fiction.   2. Large type books.
  I. Title.   II. Thorndike Press large print Candlelight series.
PS3566.R273C79 2005
  813′.54—dc22   2005022260

To Marcia Markland of Avalon Books
for her encouragement and support

and

My husband and my mother
for being my best fans

and

Marty Ambrose
for her savvy and sage advice

and

Dorothy Lampitt,
whose real-life "Loony Louie"
always made me smile

National Association for Visually Handicapped
-------------------------- *serving the partially seeing*

As the Founder/CEO of NAVH, the only national health agency solely devoted to those who, although not totally blind, have an eye disease which could lead to serious visual impairment, I am pleased to recognize Thorndike Press★ as one of the leading publishers in the large print field.

Founded in 1954 in San Francisco to prepare large print textbooks for partially seeing children, NAVH became the pioneer and standard setting agency in the preparation of large type.

Today, those publishers who meet our standards carry the prestigious "Seal of Approval" indicating high quality large print. We are delighted that Thorndike Press is one of the publishers whose titles meet these standards. We are also pleased to recognize the significant contribution Thorndike Press is making in this important and growing field.

Lorraine H. Marchi, L.H.D.
Founder/CEO
NAVH

★ Thorndike Press encompasses the following imprints: Thorndike, Wheeler, Walker and Large Print Press.

Chapter One

It is difficult to know at what moment love begins; it is less difficult to know that it has begun.

— Henry Wadsworth Longfellow

It was softly snowing at 5:30 a.m. that mid-November morning as Kayla Quinn trekked across the parking lot of the Crystal Palace sports complex toward the large arena that housed the complex's skating rink.

The pungent scent of wood smoke that hung in the air reminded Kayla of New Hampshire and the winters she'd spent there as a child. The sprawling city of Colorado Springs, where she now lived and trained, sometimes seemed worlds away from the rural countryside she thought of as home. Though she'd finally adjusted to the fast pace of city life, the sudden pang of nostalgia that gripped her heart made her realize that her loyalties still lay in the thickly forested hills and green valleys of her native state.

On the steps leading up to the arena, Kayla paused and looked back. Her eyes scanned the lot for any sign of her partner's red BMW. The only vehicles visible in the vast lot were her Plymouth Neon and the security guard's black Bronco. In the almost five years that she and Ryan Maxwell had been skating together, Kayla could recall only once when he had beaten her to the rink for an early morning practice.

Kayla shifted the pair of skates and knapsack that she had flung over her shoulder and turned to knock on one of the wood-framed glass doors that fronted the arena.

The door swung open before her hand made contact with the wood. "Hello, Sunshine." Charlie Adams, the husky security guard, gave her his standard greeting.

"Hi, Charlie." Kayla smiled, but the guard must have sensed that it was a little forced.

"Hey, are you all right?"

The man possessed an uncanny knack for picking up on any subtle change in her mood. "Fine," she said. "Just a bit chilly."

Charlie's mouth curved in a smile. "If this nasty weather's getting to you, I have the ticket. Your favorite, in fact. Espresso." He walked to his desk and with a flourish produced a tiny cup filled with the dark coffee.

"How do you do it, Charlie?" She saw no sign of an espresso machine.

He winked. "My secret."

"You're spoiling me, you know."

"If that's what you call it, I plead guilty. After all you and Ryan have done for Shelly, you deserve a lot more spoiling."

Kayla smiled over the rim of her cup. Shelly, the guard's eight-year-old daughter, was one of the members of the newly formed Crystal Palace Skating Club. The club had evolved from the skating clinic that Kayla and Ryan had been conducting for the kids on Saturdays at the arena. "I'd like to think we're helping the kids in some way," she said.

"You're doing a heap of good. Around the dinner table these days, none of the rest of us can get a word in edgewise with Shelly. She's a regular talker now. And what she says is, 'Watch what Kayla taught me.' Then she jumps up and starts into her routine. It's all her mom and I can do to get her to eat her meal." He chuckled.

"Shelly's wonderful, a joy to teach." Kayla recalled Charlie's remark that Shelly was the shy one among his three children, the one who'd always held back when her younger brother or older sister plunged feet first into some new activity. That was, until the first time he'd brought her to the arena and she'd watched Kayla and Ryan skate. "Ryan deserves most of the credit for any good that's come out of the clinic and club," she said. "They were his ideas."

Charlie crossed his arms over his ample stomach. "Ryan's plenty special. You both are." He patted the chair beside his desk. "Sit down and finish your espresso."

Kayla dropped her knapsack and skates on the floor beside the chair and sat down. "How's Joan?" She asked the question because she'd heard the guard's wife was having a tough time with her latest pregnancy — and to deflect the praise that Charlie seemed determined to lavish on her.

"Not so great. But don't worry." He beamed at her. "She wouldn't miss the Golden Skates for anything. And Doc Stevens said she should be over the morning sickness soon."

"That *is* good news." Kayla knew the couple had a special reason for wanting to be in the stands on the final night of the upcoming Golden Skates competition. Shelly and the other club members would be part of the production number that would mark the grand finale of the evening.

"None of us can wait to watch you and Ryan grab that top prize in the competition," said Charlie.

Kayla averted her gaze. "I wish I could be as confident of that as you are, Charlie." If she were truthful, confidence had been in short supply lately.

"Hey." The guard tapped the sleeve of her jacket with his hand. "You and Ryan are dynamite together. You skate like you're going to set the ice on fire."

Set the ice on fire. Once she would have believed those words were true. A year ago, she and Ryan had come very close to taking the title in the Golden Skates. They'd lost by two-tenths of a point to the then reigning national champions, Brent Stratton and Susan Lamore. Now she and Ryan were the national pairs champions. This was supposed to be their year to shine. "I hope you're right," she said.

"I know I'm right." Charlie cleared his throat. "I realize it's none of my business, but I couldn't help noticing how well you two hit it off and I was thinkin' that after you win at Worlds, maybe . . . well, you and Ryan ought to become a permanent team."

Kayla rose from her chair so fast that the contents of her cup almost spilled onto her lap. "I'm sorry, Charlie, but I need to get to practice."

"Careful, Sunshine." The guard's face was crimson. "I apologize. I talk too much."

"No," she hastened to assure him. "It's all right." Turning away, she told herself that Charlie had meant well. How could he know that after Worlds there was little chance she and Ryan would ever skate together again?

"No! No! No!"

At the brusque reprimand, Kayla came to an abrupt stop beside Ryan in the middle of the rink. His hand dropped away from her waist. Glancing up, she caught the look of chagrin on his face and turned to see their coach, Eve Baker, charging across the ice.

Eve ground to a halt in front of them,

sending a shower of ice chips flying around her ankles. "Where is the unison? Where's the passion?" she demanded. Her hands sliced the air in a flurry of emphatic gestures.

The tiny trim blond was known for speaking with her hands as much as with her mouth. The running joke among her skaters was that if someone wanted to silence her, all he need do was tie her hands behind her back.

Kayla thought the drastic measure might be worth a try. A swift glance at Ryan's expression showed her that if he had a piece of rope, he might be inclined to hang himself with it.

"Well?" Eve's green eyes glittered brightly. "You commissioned the music for this program." Her index finger shot out in Ryan's direction. "You choreographed it." Another jab of her finger punctuated the point. "So what's the problem?"

Dead quiet followed. Ryan hung his head, and a stray lock of his black wavy hair tumbled onto his brow. Kayla had to stifle the impulse to reach out and smooth the lock back in place.

What was the problem? Eve posed the question that had been hounding Kayla for weeks. Something was very wrong. And

today, from the second that she and Ryan had taken the ice and missed their first-throw double axel — a move they could almost do with their eyes closed — their routine had been a disaster. Kayla was beginning to suspect she knew the reason why, but wisdom dictated that she'd better hold her tongue until she and Ryan were alone.

"All right," Eve said. She clasped her arms in front of her.

Kayla watched as Ryan raised his eyes to meet the coach's, and she became a spectator to the minor power play going on between the two.

"Then you'll arrive at some answers, Ryan. You're aware that the judges will be observing your next practice."

"Don't worry, Eve," he said. "We'll get it together."

"I'm glad to hear that." Eve gave a slight nod of recognition and stretched her hand to touch Ryan's arm. "You look beat. You should go home and rest. That goes for both of you." Her sweeping gesture took in Kayla, but her gaze honed in on Ryan. "I want to see you in my office after lunch. Alone." With that, she turned and skated off.

Kayla stared after the coach. Eve was

tough, but she possessed great integrity, too. The combination had helped more than a few of her students aspire to national and world titles — and win them. Eve was the reason Kayla and Ryan had moved to Colorado Springs. After they had teamed together, they'd agreed that they wanted Eve as their coach, and when she relocated to the city three years ago, they had followed her. But some of her students had become casualties, dismissed by the coach for a lack of discipline. Kayla wondered now if she and Ryan were about to be given the royal boot.

"What're you thinking, Kayla?"

Searching her partner's face, she was shocked to discover purple smudges in the hollows above his cheekbones. "Not here, Ryan." She motioned him over to the boards.

"Okay, so what's up?" he asked.

Ryan leaned against the boards. Behind him a sign read *For good health, drink Spa Sparkling Mineral Water.* Despite his rugged handsomeness, his tightly toned body, he might do well to heed the sign's advice, Kayla thought. "Are you feeling all right?" she asked. She reached out to him, but he inched away from her.

"Sure. Maybe a little tired."

She brought her hand up again with the purpose of pointing out the circles under his eyes. But he turned and her fingers struck only thin air. He was withdrawing from her in that same irritating way she'd noticed of late. Once she would have shrugged off his actions as nothing more than a case of nerves. But with the competition just weeks away, his increasing moodiness was starting to try her patience. Which led to the matter she wanted to discuss with him. "I'm wondering if the problem isn't that you and Christy are burning the candle at both ends these days."

The telltale darkening of his expression told her she'd hit a sore spot. Good. Maybe he'd needed to hear that.

"I've never let my personal life interfere with my professional one," he said tersely.

"Perhaps not . . . until now. It's no secret on the tour that Christy lives to party."

Ryan's eyes pinned hers. "Are you saying that I'd risk jeopardizing your career for a good time with Christy?"

"I've never thought that," she countered, lifting her chin. *But you obviously don't know the dangers of getting involved with a woman like Christy Michaels,* she wanted to tell him, *no matter how experi-*

enced you imagine yourself to be with the opposite sex.

"So what's causing the circles under *your* eyes?" he challenged.

"What?" Where did he get the uncanny knack for always managing to turn the tables on her?

"Is someone keeping *you* out late?"

"Not someone," she retorted. "Dozens of men." There, that should silence him. Now if they could only figure out a remedy for their woes on the ice as easily as they could get into a war of words.

"Truce then, Kayla?"

The softly spoken question caught her by surprise. She met her partner's smile with a slightly grudging one of her own. "Fine. Truce, Ryan." The two of them had hit on the small ritual near the beginning of their partnership after they'd butted heads over a change in a long program. It seemed that the ritual was fast becoming a part of their daily routine.

Music suddenly blared over the arena's P.A. system, and Kayla jumped in response. She noticed then that other skaters were circling the ice. She gave an inner sigh of relief when she saw that Christy wasn't among them.

"I'm going home, Kayla. You should, too."

She looked back, and Ryan's gaze connected with hers. But before she could come up with a response, he skated off.

You're a maddening man, Ryan Maxwell. And too darned handsome for your own good. Kayla would be the first to admit that he was a treat to watch in his dark blue warm-up suit, speeding across the ice. Any female would be bound to admire the way the fabric clung to every finely chiseled muscle of his body. No wonder that he was known on the tour as "The Heartbreaker" — though, in truth, he'd suffered his share of heartbreak, too.

Observing him, Kayla recalled the beginning of their relationship as partners. She'd been an immature kid of sixteen while Ryan had been twenty-three and a definite man of the world. Talk about a mismatch! He'd barely tolerated her, had avoided her as much as possible when they were off the ice. To get even, she'd shamelessly sought out every opportunity to embarrass him by latching onto him in public places where they were sure to be seen. At the same time she'd harbored a terrible crush on him — until she'd sternly reminded herself that there was no place in her life for foolish daydreams of romance with her partner.

She could safely say now that they never would have put up with each other except for one thing. They made magic together on the ice. The chemistry kicked in as soon as their skates hit the ice. Thankfully, they were smart enough to leave it there when the music stopped. Eve had recognized their compatibility at once, and the crowds generally went crazy over their performances — whether they were competing for the national championship or skating an exhibition in a drafty coliseum in Cleveland.

Over the years they had forged a bond of friendship and respect for each other. She came to learn that he hadn't had an easy childhood. His father had abruptly asked for a divorce when Ryan was ten and had paid little or no attention to his son after that. Once, with what looked suspiciously like a tear gleaming in his eye, Ryan had told her that his father had never come to watch him skate in a competition, that he was out of Ryan's life altogether within a year of the divorce. It was then she had confessed to Ryan that it had taken the shock of losing her parents in a car crash when she was thirteen to seal her determination to skate with a professional touring company. Her parents had made so many sacrifices so that her dreams might come true. Now at twenty-one, she was on the threshold of achieving those dreams. And she and Ryan were . . .

"Ah, so how is the fair half of the dynamic, dark-haired duo today?"

Kayla gasped and steeled herself to meet the coarse, angular face of Fletcher Godwin. "Perfect, Fletcher." She made herself return his gaze. "But you don't look well."

The deposed men's singles champion gifted her with a frigid smile. "Oh, I'm very well. But I saw you arguing with that devilish rogue of a partner of yours."

Fletcher's tongue cut like the sharp blades of his skates. His pride in his half-British ancestry was well known, and word had it that he'd harbored hopes of becoming a Shakespearean actor. Too bad he'd taken up skating instead. "Sorry," she said. "You're mistaken."

"I fear the lady doth protest too much."

I'm not the only one, Kayla almost told him. She hated his condescending attitude. Six months before, he'd become one of Eve's casualties, and since then he seemed to be getting his kicks from tormenting Kayla and her partner at every convenient opportunity. It would be just like him to have watched their disastrous practice session. He loved gathering fodder for the circuit's gossip mill.

Fletcher moved in closer. "What a pity. Can't come up with an excuse for the poor man, can you?"

"That," she snapped, "doesn't dignify a response." She put her back to him and headed for the exit.

Bent on increasing the distance between herself and Fletcher, she blindly ignored the other skaters whizzing past her. Until one of them loomed in front of her like a blurry white tree. Kayla stabbed at the ice with her right toe pick in a frantic attempt to stop. But it was too late. She cried out a warning and threw her hands up to shield herself from the inevitable collision. Just as quickly, someone grabbed hold of her and yanked her aside. Blinking, she saw a fuzzy halo of curly red hair. "Meghan?" Her best friend's face came into focus. Meghan Sommers's blue eyes were wide with fright.

"What happened over there between you and Fletcher?"

Kayla shook her head. "Just up to his old tricks."

Meghan's freckled nose wrinkled in distaste. "The man is nuts — a true basket case."

"Don't forget God's gift to the world of skating."

Meghan looped her arm through Kayla's. "Why don't we discuss it over croissants at the café?"

"Sounds good to me."

It was while they were changing from their skates to their shoes that Kayla thought to ask, "By the way, who did I nearly send to the hospital?"

"You didn't feel the daggers Christy shot at you?"

Kayla moaned. "Wonderful. I come within a hair's breadth of knocking my partner's girlfriend senseless."

"And my chief competition, don't forget."

Laughter suddenly bubbled up in Kayla's throat. It was a healthy release of the tension that had been building all day, she told herself. There wasn't anything funny about her near mishap with Christy.

But then Meghan began to laugh, too, and their spirits were still high as they crossed the street from the arena to the Palace Café.

The small restaurant was almost exclusively a skaters' hangout, the spot where many of them congregated between practices. It was also a place where business was conducted and contracts hashed out over a meal of eggs Benedict and home-fried potatoes. And a place where romance bloomed, Kayla was reminded when she spied Scott Beckman lounging in one of the café's high-backed wooden booths. Scott was the reigning men's singles champion — and the love of Meghan's life. Meghan was fond of telling how they'd fallen for each other over a piece of apple pie they'd shared at the café. "It was love at first bite," she often joked.

A twinge of envy twisted through Kayla. She'd never seen Meghan happier than she was now. Scott's infectious, slightly lop-sided smile told her that he was happy, too. She was glad for her friends. Then why on earth did the fact they were in love make her feel uncomfortable?

"I'll see you this afternoon," Meghan murmured to Scott.

"Okay, Meggy."

"How's it going, Kayla?" Scott touched her arm.

"Fine, Scott." He must have seen through her transparency; the boyish smile faded to a frown. She was grateful when Meghan chose that moment to steer her toward a booth at the back of the restaurant.

After the waitress had taken their order of coffee and croissants, Meghan leaned her elbows on the table. "So, what's up with you and Ryan these days?"

"I thought we were discussing Fletcher."

"We already know what's up with him." Meghan grinned. "Besides, he really isn't the problem, is he?"

Spoken in typical blunt Meghan fashion. Kayla unfolded her napkin and placed it in her lap. Then she set to rearranging her knife, fork, and spoon so that they would be in perfect alignment with one another. All the while she was aware that Meghan was watching her.

"You want everything in your life to be orderly and well arranged, don't you?" Meghan said.

"What's wrong with that?" Kayla asked too sharply. She sighed. "I'm sorry. I've just been so edgy these last weeks. I wish I could tell you what's up with Ryan and me. Suddenly we're acting like a couple of . . ." She made a pretext of examining her knife for smudges. "What I mean is that our practices are a mess. In case you hadn't noticed."

"You think Ryan's involvement with Christy is to blame."

Kayla had to smile at her friend's insight.

"Since he's been dating her, he's . . . he's changed."

"His mind's too much on the party girl and not enough on his routines?"

"Do you have a better idea?"

Meghan lifted a delicate eyebrow. "Maybe."

"What —"

The waitress appeared at that instant with their order. "In your opinion, Dr. Meg," Kayla said when the waitress was gone, "what's ailing the team of Quinn and Maxwell?"

Meghan dabbed butter on her croissant. "Let's just say I have a couple of theories."

"Theories? What kind of a diagnosis is that?"

"The best one I can give you at the moment." Meghan took a tiny bite of the croissant. She always seemed to more nibble at her food than eat it. "I have every faith that you and Ryan will sweep the competition at the Golden Skates. Inspiration will come, Kayla, when you least expect it. I'd bet my own championship on it."

"Careful. The big night'll soon be on us."

"And speaking of the big night, I'm due back at the rink in two minutes. Unfortunately for me, Christy doesn't appear to be suffering from distractions these days, despite her preoccupation with a certain hunky pairs skater."

"Have you noticed the way she hangs all over him?"

Meghan wrinkled her nose. "Like a vine." She got up from the booth and took a couple of quick swallows of coffee from her cup. "Ouch. Hot!" She fanned her tongue, then wrapped her uneaten croissant in a napkin. "Coming?"

"Thanks, but I think I'll stay and spare my tongue the burns." Her attempt at humor was met with a slightly withering glance. "Eve canceled practice until this afternoon. She sent Ryan home to rest. I'm supposed to be resting, too."

"Rest?" Meghan looked skeptical. "So see you at dinner then? Scott found this new place called the Pizza Connection that has a fabulous salad bar *and* a live country-and-western band."

A live band. That meant loud music and a large crowd. "I'm not sure I can make it."

"No? Most of the gang'll be wandering in around six."

Ryan and Christy were sure to show. Likely Fletcher too. "I may just cook dinner at home."

Meghan studied her for a moment. "Okay. If you change your mind, we'll save a place for you." She turned and, with a wave of her hand, headed for the register at the front of the café.

Kayla shut her eyes and massaged her temples. It was only the middle of the morning and already every muscle in her body screamed with fatigue. Maybe Ryan had the right idea; she should have gone home. Her conversation with Meghan certainly hadn't lightened her mood. If anything, she felt more confused.

Common sense told Kayla that she couldn't expect her friend to come up with some profound answer that would solve Quinn and Maxwell's woes on the ice. But Meghan hinted that she had a couple of theories as to what was wrong. So why was she being so cagey about them?

Chapter Two

Ryan shifted his weight, hitching one leg over the other. Seated across from Eve in her cubbyhole of an office, he'd spent the better part of the past thirty minutes under her scrutiny. Their conversation had been mostly about trivial matters — a small change she wanted in the long program he and Kayla would be skating in the competition; a discussion of the pair's final costume fitting and whether a white stripe should be added to each outer leg seam of his black tux outfit. All the while, Ryan had the feeling that Eve was acting more and more like a tigress on a hunt, biding her time until she could catch her prey off-guard.

The tigress regarded him now, a slight smile on her lips. "Don't forget. The club members will be trying on their costumes tomorrow, too, at Estelle's."

"I haven't forgotten." He tried to imagine the scene in Estelle Lampitt's tiny shoebox of a shop with seven kids squirming and giggling and all vying for the seamstress's attention at the same time. The idea brought a grin to his mouth — until he met his coach's eyes again.

Eve had taken a pen from a drawer and set it on top of her desk. While he watched, she reached for a stack of papers that occupied a nearby file cabinet. She shuffled the pile, plucked out one of the sheets of paper, and laid it beside the pen. "Did you rest?" she asked.

"Sure, Eve." *What a joke,* he thought, untangling his legs and planting his feet squarely on the floor. Rest had been the last thing on his mind when he'd gone home.

"Do I detect a note of sarcasm?"

Ryan clamped his jaw tight and ran a hand impatiently through his hair.

"I believe I know what the problem is," she said.

Her tone of voice commanded his attention. Their gazes locked across the desk. "I'm glad to hear you have it figured out," he said.

"It's very simple." She folded her busy hands together in front of her. "The problem is that you're afraid."

She was obviously joking — or trying to

rile him. He didn't bother to respond.

But Eve didn't look as if she were joking. "I don't think you recognize your own magnetism, Ryan. If you wanted them, you could charm the stripes off a zebra."

"And glue them on my tux?"

"Marvelous sense of humor, too, but I believe we both know the real subject here is women. Kayla and Christy, to be exact."

Ryan groaned inwardly. "Are you saying that I have some strange fear of two of the most important women in my life?" Judging by the expression on the tigress's face, maybe he should have made that three.

"Not *of* them. I'd say you're more afraid of what you perceive as a conflict in your relationships with Kayla and Christy. Though I could be wrong — I pray that I am — I would guess that's what is distracting you and interfering with your concentration at practice."

"There's no conflict in my relationships. Kayla's my partner and a good friend. Christy's the woman I'm dating at the moment." Why couldn't the coach get the point? It was simple logic. "It isn't as if I've lived the life of a monk these past few years. I'd say I've dated a respectable number of women."

"Of course you have, Ryan." Eve gifted him with a smile. "Your manhood is not in question. But I wonder if you've noticed how much Kayla has changed in those same few years. She's matured into a lovely young woman, one who possesses a great deal of strength and inner beauty."

Ryan stared out the tiny window of the office. The view framed in the pane of glass was of a naked tree limb set against a gray sky. Did the coach think he was blind? Sure, he'd seen Kayla's beauty blossom like some rare, exotic flower coming into its glory.

The sound of a pen scratching on paper brought Ryan's attention back to Eve. She was drawing something on the piece of paper she'd set aside earlier. When she was finished, she handed the sheet to Ryan for his inspection.

Ryan peered at the large, plain triangle Eve had drawn. His name was written at the top apex of the figure, with Kayla's and Christy's scribbled opposite each other at the base. "What's this, Eve? A love triangle?"

"You tell me."

Apparently, the charm Eve had spoken of moments ago hadn't worked its effects on her. "Are you trying to say I'd risk getting romantically involved with my partner? No way, Eve. That'd be crazy. Besides, I learned my lesson on that score years ago." A plenty painful lesson that haunted him to this day.

"I realize you were hurt when Gillian didn't return your feelings. And that you blamed yourself for the breakup of your partnership."

Ryan passed a hand over his eyes. *Gillian.* Memories of his former partner stabbed like a knife at his heart. He *was* to blame for their breakup. If he hadn't fallen for her, hadn't carried his passion for her off the ice and into her living room that cold winter night after they'd won big at regionals, chances were they would still be partners. *And Gillian's talent wouldn't have gone down the tubes,* he thought with fresh agony.

"You know," Eve was saying, "some of the greatest pairs skaters have become couples off the ice as well as on. Often, things work out well. Then sometimes they don't."

Ryan barely heard the coach's words. He was remembering the cheers of the audience, the happy smile on Gillian's face the night they had won at Eastern Regionals in Bangor. *Has it really been almost seven years ago?* he asked himself. In his mind's eye, he saw himself and Gillian, standing in the center of that lighted patch of ice, soaking up the admiration of the crowd.

He cleared his throat. "I don't plan to go down that road again," he said, unable to keep the huskiness from his voice. He savagely crumpled the piece of paper in his hand and shoved it in his jeans pocket. "We all know what my goals are in relation to the team of Quinn and Maxwell."

"Yes, but I wonder if you're not selling yourself short."

He shook his head. "My future was sealed when I took that fall and cracked up my knee and shinbone. With every tumble on the ice, I've punished the knee a little more." He didn't mention that the pain had worsened of late, that it served as a constant reminder of how fast his days as a competitive skater were running out. "Kayla has a fantastic future ahead of her. I've got to do what's best for her." *And I'm prepared to do whatever it takes to make sure she reaches her goals.* "As for me," he said aloud, "my future's set, too. I'll be joining the coaching team at Bill's rink."

Bill Brenner, his former coach, had given him his start in figure skating. When Kayla's former partner had to quit the sport to care for family obligations, Bill had been instrumental in encouraging Ryan to give pairs skating another try with her.

It was Bill's club, the Maple Leafs, out of Winding River, New York, that gave Ryan the inspiration to set up the Crystal Palace Club. Bill had established the Maple Leafs to help talented kids from low-income families. Ryan had been one of the skaters who'd benefited from Bill's generosity, particularly after his parents' divorce when his father had copped out on child support payments and fled the state for who knew where.

"Did Bill put a time limit on his offer?" Eve asked.

"I've made a commitment to him," Ryan hedged. *A commitment I mean to keep.* "I plan to move to Winding River right after Worlds."

Ryan recalled the last time he'd seen Bill. It had been during the week of Nationals close to a year ago. *"A job's waiting for you, Ryan,"* the coach had said over breakfast one morning. *"Just got a promising new skater. Name's Todd Connors. Ten years old and full of enthusiasm. You'd be the ideal coach for him."*

"What about the club here?"

"How's that, Eve? Oh . . . the club. Scott'll be taking over from me. He'll do a great job. He's terrific with the kids."

"So are you and Kayla."

"Yeah, well . . ." Ryan made a show of checking his watch. "Speaking of Kayla, she'll be waiting for me at the rink." It seemed a good excuse for ending his conversation with the coach. "If there isn't anything else . . ."

"Nothing else, except you do realize that you almost let Kayla fall this morning on that first double axel?"

Did Eve have to remind him? Ryan pushed back his chair and stood up. "It won't happen again."

"A parting thought, Ryan."

He'd had enough of those, but out of deference to his coach, he stopped short of the door. "What's that?"

"Don't be too hard on yourself if everything doesn't work out quite like you're expecting it to."

Not about to ask what she meant by that statement, he strode from her office, pulling the door shut as he went. Once he was out of Eve's sight, he slowed his steps. The long corridor housed all of the coaches' offices. The doors on either side were closed, and he found himself alone in the hallway.

Ryan slouched against the wall and tried to collect his thoughts. The whole conversation with Eve had been a waste of time, and the coach had been way off base in her estimation of his relationship with his partner.

Naturally, he couldn't deny that he found Kayla attractive. She'd definitely grown up during the several years they'd been a team. What warm-blooded male wouldn't occasionally entertain a desire to run his hands through that long, shiny dark hair of hers, or let himself get lost for a while in those lush brown eyes? And what man wouldn't fantasize now and again about tasting the sweetness of those generous, slightly pouty lips?

Ryan had thought of all of those things, and a time or two recently he'd even allowed himself to dwell for a brief moment on the idea of kissing his partner. Not one of those pecks that he planted on her forehead or cheek whenever they won a competition, but a deep, lingering kiss.

He shook himself mentally. *Remember, pal, you promised yourself you're never going down that road again.* And he'd learned his lessons well, knew enough to keep himself under tight control and rein in his imagination before it could cut loose like a runaway train. Not only that. He had a great working relationship with Kayla — the kind he'd had with Gillian before he'd let his feelings get the better of his good judgment. He wasn't about to betray his partner, throw their friendship to the four winds.

Still, he had to admit that Eve had been onto something. He wasn't his usual self. And it was more than his worry over whether his bum knee would hold out through Worlds. He felt way too restless, as if ants were doing the jitterbug under his skin. His weird moods had to be affecting his performance on the ice, even if he wanted to deny it.

Maybe Kayla was right after all. He and Christy had been keeping some pretty wild hours recently, and most nights when his head finally hit the pillow, he ended up doing more tossing and turning than sleeping.

Wasn't the solution smack in front of his eyes? The fact was he'd just have to be upfront with Christy, tell her that he had to curtail the partying for a while.

His mind made up on the matter, Ryan started in the direction of the locker rooms. Female voices coming from the far end of the hall brought him to a fast halt.

When he recognized the one with the high-pitched laugh as Christy's, he walked quickly in the other direction. He wasn't ready at the moment to encounter that particular important woman in his life. Not with the tigress Eve's lecture still burning in his ears. And not when he was headed out to meet the woman who shared his dream of capturing the pairs title in the Golden Skates.

The judges sat together in the stands one tier above the rink. From Kayla's perspective on the ice, the four men and three women resembled sharp-eyed hawks lined up in a row. The image caused a nervous flutter in her stomach. It was common knowledge that judges almost ruled the world of competitive skating. A gesture as innocent as a frown or a raised eyebrow on a judge's part could send a skater into a frenzy of self-recrimination for two-footing a jump or taking an unexpected fall on the ice.

Kayla knew four of the seven judges well, and she had to wonder what their assessment of Quinn and Maxwell would be after today's practice. Would their faces set in a collective frown of dismay? Or would they have cause to smile and nod their heads in approval? The flutter in her stomach became a knot, and she wished Ryan would come.

Scott Beckman was scheduled to skate first. When the beginning notes of his music blared over the public address, Kayla turned toward the ice. She had no doubt that he would skate a clean program. Meghan had confided that he was up for the competition, hungry to prove that his win at Nationals wasn't a fluke, and that Fletcher's prediction of a comeback was so much hot air.

Watching him, Kayla thought, *How can he lose when he has Meghan's love to inspire him?* He certainly didn't look like a loser, if his opening triple Lutz was any indication. With a killer smile on his face, he charged down the ice and nailed a double toe loop, then a triple axel. Enthusiastic applause broke out from the small band of spectators that shared the stands with the judges. Kayla searched the stands until she found Meghan seated in the tier to the left of the judges. She caught her friend's attention, and the two of them exchanged smiles and victory signs.

But Kayla's smile vanished the moment she looked away. If only she could be as certain of her own performance — and of

Ryan's — as she was of Scott's. Though she hadn't seen Ryan since they'd parted that morning, her mind had been preoccupied with thoughts of him, and she'd grown more and more curious about what Eve had wanted to discuss with him. Had the coach come down hard on him about his relationship with Christy? Or maybe she had . . .

"Hi."

Kayla made a sharp turn and came face-to-face with her partner. "Hi, yourself," she said. One glance at Ryan's expression warned her off of asking any questions about the infamous meeting with the coach. She consoled herself by thinking that he looked less exhausted than when he'd gone home. He also managed to look unbearably handsome in his tight black leather pants and checked satin shirt.

"Hey, what's the matter?" he asked.

"Mmm." Kayla blinked. "Nothing," she said. What *was* the matter with her, staring at him like that, admiring how snugly his pants fit his legs, noticing the rippling of his muscles under the satin fabric of his shirt? Hadn't she seen him in the costume at least a dozen times? It complemented her dress of white chiffon, and they'd chosen the outfits to wear to practice that afternoon because they resembled the ones they'd be wearing in the competition. Judges appreciated details like that. So why all of a sudden was she thinking there was something different about his appearance — as if his sex appeal had jumped several degrees since she'd last seen him in the costume?

"Have you warmed up yet?" he said.

"Warm? Yes, it's a little warm in here . . ." Ryan's laughter brought her to her senses, and she began to look away from him. But her gaze was arrested by the shadow of doubt that clouded the chocolate-brown depths of his eyes. His laughter faded away. *What's wrong?* she thought. She touched his arm, grasping for some witty remark that would bring back his smile.

But he stepped aside from her and gazed up at the stands. "We'd better get started," he said. Without warning, he took off like a rocket across the ice, and she nearly tripped over her own feet trying to keep up with him. They skated in strained silence to the other end of the rink where Eve stood waiting for them.

The coach appeared to be in an upbeat mood. She clasped one arm around Kayla, the other around Ryan. "A simple piece of advice. Think only of skating your best and be conservative since you're both a little uncertain today. Keep in mind that the judges might forgive a less than perfect double axel, but they're not going to forget if you fall on a toe loop." She directed a smile at each of them, adding, "Don't worry. You'll do fine."

Easy for you to say, thought Kayla as she forced a smile for Eve's sake. She wondered that the coach didn't feel the tension building in the air. It hummed around herself and her partner like wire buzzing in a stiff breeze. Was it only due to the fact that they both badly wanted to skate a perfect program? Or was there some deeper cause? Kayla had no time to ponder over the matter. The clock was inching toward 3:00 p.m.

Scott finished his program to a hearty round of applause. The next music to come over the P.A. would be the jazzy piece Ryan had commissioned for the beginning part of their long program.

"Ten minutes to go, Kayla."

Did Ryan have to remind her? Glancing at him, she noted he had the defeated look of a man about to face a firing squad. "Are you okay?"

"Never been better."

Should she hope for a miracle? Unless

things turned around fast for them, they might need one.

"Why don't we give it a practice shot?" he suggested.

Kayla's heart faltered, skipped a beat. "I'm ready," he said, though "ready" was a dubious word at the moment.

She told herself that if she landed her first double axel, and they managed to complete their side-by-side triple toe loops without a fall, they might skate a decent program, if not an exciting one. But the idea failed to comfort her.

They circled the ice, building up speed before moving into position for the throw double axel. Then the unthinkable happened. Kayla froze, her muscles betraying her. "No, Ryan!"

He was ahead of her, slowing their pace. "Why did you freeze out there?" he asked, guiding her to the boards. His eyes were dark pools of concern.

"I don't know." She wanted to kick herself for making a tense situation worse. Panic rose inside her. She summoned every ounce of willpower, and finally the panic began to subside. She wasn't used to her body betraying her. Hadn't she learned long ago to keep a firm grip on her emotions? So what was happening? Why did she feel as if she were falling apart when she needed most to be in control of her faculties?

"Take a few deep breaths," Ryan instructed.

She did as he ordered, inhaling, holding, exhaling. Her muscles relaxed a little. "I'm all right," she said, not looking up for fear she would catch Eve watching her.

"Okay, one minute and we're on," Ryan said softly. He took her hand in his and gently squeezed her fingers. Then he guided her to the center of the rink.

They stood facing the judges when the first bars of their music came on. The program began with a saxophone solo, sophisticated and sensual in tone. The smoky notes filled the arena, but the only thing Kayla heard was the voice in her head that chanted, *Land the double, land the double.* She and Ryan cut a path across the ice. He lifted her into position for the throw; she caught her breath as she felt herself being hurled high in the air.

Land the double. She spun in the air for two and a half revolutions and executed a perfect landing on the blade of her right skate. The sound of applause echoed in her ears, and she acknowledged it with a smile.

They gathered speed again, then separated and launched into their side-by-side triple toe loops. Kayla made another flawless landing. From the shouts of the crowd, so had her partner. After that, she recalled only snatches of their program. Muscle memory took over, and by the time they went into their final sit spin, Kayla knew they had skated well. Maybe not passionately. Nor brilliantly. But well enough, she reasoned, to please the judges. And that was what counted.

Kayla felt the whisper of a kiss against her hair, and she glanced up to find Ryan smiling down at her. *We did it,* his eyes telegraphed to hers.

After they'd taken their bows, they skated back to Eve. The coach looked happy. "The press is waiting for you," she announced. "Outside in the corridor."

Kayla's heart sank. She wasn't in the mood at the moment to meet the press.

"Why don't we slip out the side door?" Ryan suggested.

Eve gave a sardonic laugh. "Not a good idea." Those green eyes brooked no argument. "Since neither Lamore and Stratton nor the Kapinskys will be in town until competition week, you two are center stage. Take advantage of it."

The coach had a point, Kayla grudgingly admitted. The Golden Skates was a showcase for local talent, but skaters from all over the country clamored to participate in the prestigious event. Lamore and Stratton were sure to garner attention when they stormed into town, ready to avenge the loss of their national title. And the Kapinskys, the third-ranked pair in the United States, were notorious for wooing the judges with their high-energy routines.

"I think we could spare a few minutes for the press. Don't you, Ryan?"

He smiled, but it was a tired smile. "As long as it's only a few."

"Then go," Eve said. She passed them their skate guards and chased them off with a wave of her hand.

The press turned out to be a reporter and a cameraman from the more popular of the two local TV stations. The reporter was an attractive young woman with a perky smile and perfect diction. And a crush on Ryan, it appeared to Kayla. The woman's gaze kept roving back to him as she asked questions from a clipboard in her hands.

The questions were standard ones. Were they pleased with their performance? Did they plan to make changes in their program? Lamore and Stratton lost their national title. Were Quinn and Maxwell confident they could steal the Golden Skates crown away from the current champions?

Ryan's answers were as routine as the questions, but Kayla was growing more than a little peeved with the reporter's tactics. The woman was flirting outrageously with Ryan. *So why should I care?* Kayla asked herself. Women were always throwing themselves at Ryan, weren't they? On occasion the tables were even turned and Kayla found herself the object of a good-looking male reporter's attentions. But for some reason, she wasn't in the mood to put up with coy TV sportscasters.

At last the interview came to an end. That didn't stop the woman from keeping up her patter with Ryan. At the same time, she turned her back on Kayla, and whatever exchange went on between the two was lost on her. The next thing Kayla knew, Ryan was tapping her on the shoulder.

"Let's get out of here," he said.

More irked than she wanted to admit, she couldn't help asking, "Did you get her name and phone number?" His reply was a grin and a shrug, which told her nothing.

They walked without speaking to an entrance of the rink. "Are you going in?" he said, breaking the silence.

Kayla hadn't considered it. Another pair was skating that afternoon, but they were well down in the rankings. "I don't know." She paused. "Are you?"

"Have to. Christy's skating in twenty minutes."

Of course. "I doubt she'd appreciate me hanging around to cheer her on. I think I'll get a snack at the café."

"You sure?" He seemed to hesitate. "You'll be at the Pizza Connection later, won't you?"

Does it really matter to you if I'm there or not? "I don't think so. I'm . . ."

"Ah, they've kissed and made up."

Ryan spun around, bringing Kayla with him. She found herself almost nose-to-nose with Fletcher. Dressed in gaudy blue satin that was festooned with spangles and sequins, Fletcher made her think of a strutting peacock in full plumage. His gaze flickered over her partner before fixing coolly on her. "I believe the poet Shelley said it best, dear Kayla." He flung out his hand in an expansive gesture as he dropped to one knee in front of her.

" 'Oh, lift me from the grass!
I die! I faint! I fail!
Let thy love in kisses rain
On my lips and eyelids pale.
My cheek is cold and white, alas!
My heart beats loud and fast;
Oh! Press it to thine own again,
Where it will break at last.' "

Fletcher slapped his hand over his heart and bowed his head.

Meghan was right. Fletcher was crazy. But what was his point in spouting poetry? Kayla was about to ask him when Ryan's fingers clamped down on hers.

"Let's get some fresh air in our lungs," he gritted out between clenched teeth.

Before Kayla could respond to either man, Ryan pulled her away. She glanced back over her shoulder. Fletcher flashed her a smug smile.

Instead of taking her for fresh air, Ryan stopped as soon as they were out of Fletcher's sight. "I need to change my clothes before Christy's program starts." A muscle twitched in his jaw. "Why don't you reconsider about dinner," he said, then walked away.

Kayla leaned against the wall and closed her eyes. Her body felt as if it had been forced through a meat grinder. Her brain was swaddled in a fog of confusion and fatigue. Home and a hot bath sounded far more appealing than dinner at some crowded pizza joint.

On the other hand, she had to acknowledge that maybe it would do her good to be in the company of others — even if that company included Christy and Fletcher. Her social calendar had been woefully empty for weeks.

The lack of a personal life was a common hazard of the profession, one Kayla usually accepted without complaint. Between practices and competitions and performing in exhibitions, there were precious few hours left for pursuing a good time. *Or a serious relationship,* she thought, even if her partner never seemed to go begging for company from the opposite sex. But while loneliness was the usual lament among many of the skaters she knew, she had steadfastly shied away from even the idea of becoming romantically involved with someone.

She sighed, recalling the cinematographer she'd met at an exhibition in Calgary two years ago, where Ryan and she had managed to wow the audience with their interpretation of the Stevie Nicks song

"Leather and Lace."

The cinematographer had flirted with her, taken her to dinner and a couple of movies. He'd called her, even flown to the Springs to watch her skate in a competition. They'd started dating. He'd made it clear he wanted more than a casual relationship. For a giddy moment, she'd thought she wanted that, too. Until she'd come to the sobering conclusion that she couldn't make an emotional commitment to a man, only to face being separated from him for weeks or months at a stretch. Looking back, she'd been forced to realize that her fear of forming too intimate an attachment to another person was implanted in her mind the instant she'd heard the horrifying news of her parents' deaths. And from that day on, she'd begun to build walls around her heart to guard it against the possibility of ever being hurt that much again.

Still, there was another guy, a Hollywood agent, who'd wined and dined her last year when she was in L.A. He'd wired her roses, despite the fact she'd turned down his offer of representation. He'd shown her a good time, had slipped her his phone number and told her that all she need do was call and he'd be on the next flight to Colorado Springs.

She was glad, wasn't she, that she'd made a conscious choice to keep herself free from romantic entanglements? Deep inside, she knew it was the only way that she could clearly keep her goals in sight. The lucky ones, she supposed, were people like Meghan and Scott. They were both in the business; they understood the sacrifices involved in pursuing a career in skating. They could plan a future together, join the same tour when they turned pro, never have to worry about being apart for long, lonely periods of time.

Perhaps someday, thought Kayla wistfully, *I'll meet someone on the pro tour, a special man who'll sweep me off my skates and make me trust in love again.*

But why did she suddenly feel as if there were a void in her life? Was it because of Meghan and Scott? Happiness could be fleeting. *Or a cruel illusion,* she told herself.

Yet, she reasoned, it couldn't hurt to resume dating once in a while just for fun. Maybe it was time to dust off the phone number of that attentive agent and make a call to L.A.

Chapter Three

" 'Darling, love me tonight. . . .' " The female lead singer of the Bandits leaned into the microphone from the stage at the Pizza Connection.

From where she sat in a corner booth, Kayla had a clear view of the four-piece band and the tiny dance floor. She watched as Scott and Meghan and Justin and Chelsea joined the other couples on the dance floor. According to Scott, who happened to be a rabid country music fan, the Bandits were a group destined for stardom in Nashville.

Kayla could take country music or leave it, though she had to concede that the song the miniskirted blond was belting out certainly qualified as a tearjerker. She slid a glance toward the next booth, where Christy was all but perched in Ryan's lap. It was doubtful they were even aware the band was playing. On the other side of

Ryan, Mitchell Porter, an up-and-coming men's singles skater, sat nursing a beer and looking a little glum.

" '. . . just take me in your arms and everything will be all right,' " the singer crooned into the microphone.

Kayla picked at her salad, spearing a forkful of greens. The lettuce tasted stale. From the corner of her eye, she saw Christy feeding Ryan his slice of pizza.

I shouldn't have come, thought Kayla. Several of the gang were no-shows that evening — including Fletcher. Someone had said he'd gone home with a headache after missing his triple axel twice in his long program. Kayla almost wished she'd developed a headache, too. Then she'd have had a legitimate excuse for bowing out of dinner.

The blond singer brought the song to a soulful conclusion, then announced that the Bandits would be taking a short break.

"Y'all stick around now," she yelled over a loud background riff from the drummer, "because we've got a heap more music to play for y'all tonight."

Meghan and Scott returned to the booth, while Justin and Chelsea made a quick detour to the salad bar. Meghan's face was flushed — *glowing* was a better word, Kayla decided. Meghan's face seemed to glow a lot these days.

"Hey, Mitch," Scott called as soon as he was settled in the booth, "I hear you've signed up with Brookings."

The mention of the name Brookings snapped Kayla out of her reflective mood. Hamil Brookings was the agent who had sent her roses and taken her to dinner.

Mitchell put up his hand. "Nada, Scott."

"Come on," Scott retorted, "don't hold out on us."

"Honest." Mitchell grinned. "I haven't signed on the dotted line — yet. But Brookings did make me a tempting offer."

"Personally, *I* wouldn't recommend Hamil Brookings to any skater. Any skater who's *female,* that is."

Kayla grew instantly alert at the sound of Christy's voice.

"Not if she wants to keep her self-respect," Christy added. Her mouth puckered in a small frown.

Kayla bristled at the obvious inference.

"What do you mean, wants to keep her self-respect?" Justin put in.

"I mean that Hamil's an octopus. That is . . ." She lifted her long blond hair and swept it over her left shoulder. "The man can't keep his hands to himself." She set frosty eyes on Kayla. "But I'm sure no one knows that better than Kayla since she's been dating Hamil."

At that moment, Kayla considered that she could strangle Christy Michaels and not bat an eyelash. She straightened her shoulders. "Hamil's always been the perfect gentleman when he's with me," she said, surprised by the saucy tone of her voice. She noted with satisfaction that Ryan was staring stonily at his plate. But her reward from Christy was a look that could have flash-frozen the root beer in her mug.

"Say, Ryan." Mitchell gave Ryan's shoulder a tap. "Aren't you and Kayla in the market for an agent?"

Please, enough about agents for one night. Kayla noted that her sentiments were mirrored in Ryan's expression. He brought his mug of cola to his mouth and took a swallow.

"No, we're not," he said with a pointed look that should have laid the subject to rest.

Kayla caught Meghan and Scott exchanging glances, and she imagined that Scott regretted bringing up the subject.

"I've been trying to persuade him to talk to Sully." Christy plucked at the sleeve of

Ryan's shirt. Sully Vancoff, a high-powered Hollywood type, was Christy's agent. "But he's being so stubborn." Her fingers slowly stroked down his forearm. "You know you are, Ryan."

Kayla didn't hear Ryan's reply — if he made one. She was too busy trying to quell the anger that rose in her throat like bile. Hamil wasn't the only one who couldn't keep his hands to himself. Christy hadn't quit pawing at Ryan since the two of them had set foot in the restaurant. And the manipulative manner in which she tried to influence him to do her bidding. . . .

She'll ruin him yet. The nauseating idea sent a fresh rush of anger through Kayla.

"What's wrong?"

Kayla feigned a smile as Meghan's fingers wrapped around hers. "Nothing. I'm fine."

"Are you sure? You look absolutely pale."

"I just need a good night's sleep."

"I understand," Meghan said soothingly.

Kayla dropped her fork beside her plate of uneaten salad. "I'm going now. Ryan and I have an early morning practice and . . ."

"Leaving already, Kayla?"

"Yes, Mitchell. If you'll excuse me . . ."

"She's tired," Kayla heard Meghan explain.

Avoiding Scott's inquisitive glance, she slid out of the booth. "See you tomorrow," she tossed over her shoulder.

Kayla got as far as the door of the restaurant when a hand clasped hold of her arm. "Why are you going?"

"It's been a long day, Ryan."

"But you didn't finish your dinner," he said.

She turned on her heel. "I lost my appetite." Jerking away from his grasp, she yanked up the zipper on her jacket and pushed past him.

Ryan followed her outside. "Look, Kayla, sometimes Christy says things she doesn't mean. We all know that."

Kayla swung around — and found her eyes inches from his. "I have no doubt that Christy meant every word she said tonight."

A sharp gust of wind came out of nowhere, howling past the corner of the building and bringing with it a flurry of snowflakes. Before Kayla could shield herself from the wintry blast, Ryan pivoted her around so that their positions were reversed. The move served to protect her from the wind and block her exit at the same time.

Ryan jammed his hands in his jeans pockets. "Why didn't you tell me you were involved with Brookings?"

His breath, condensing in white puffs in the frigid air, warmed Kayla's cheeks. "Maybe it's because you never asked me," she flared. "Besides, what difference does it make to you who I date?"

Ryan's eyes glinted brightly in the light from a nearby post lamp. Kayla tried to read the expression in them, but failed. When he made no move to leave, she said, "You're going to turn into an icicle. Not to mention that Christy and your pizza are both getting cold."

Their gazes locked for a moment. Finally, Ryan took his hands from his pockets. He brushed a snowflake from her jacket. "Just one thing, partner," he said. His eyes narrowed. "Drive carefully." With that, he wheeled away and strode back into the restaurant.

Kayla watched him in exasperation. Christy was right about something. Ryan Maxwell was a stubborn man. But Kayla figured she could be stubborn, too. Pulling the collar of her jacket tighter against her neck, she faced into the wind and walked toward her car.

Her hand was on the door handle of her car when she heard the crunch of footsteps behind her. "Ryan . . ." She flung a hand out in frustration and spun around — only to find herself staring into the startled faces of two strangers. "I'm sorry," she stammered to the man and the woman. "I thought —"

"No." The man held up his hand. "We're sorry. We didn't mean to surprise you, Miss Quinn. It's just that, uh, we. . . ." He looked to the woman beside him; she nodded and he went on, "We apologize for bothering you in such inclement weather and all, but . . . we saw you coming from the restaurant and, uh, our daughter always watches your shows."

"For pity sakes, Edward," the woman chided, "the young woman will freeze to death while you're bumbling about. Just say it." With a gusty sigh, she turned to Kayla. "What Edward's trying to tell you is that our daughter, Celia, is a fan of yours. Could we get your autograph?"

Kayla put on as gracious a smile as she could muster given the circumstances. "Of course," she said. *Who's more embarrassed,* she wondered as she searched her purse for something to write on, *Edward or me?* She considered the disconcerting possibility that the couple had overheard the words she and Ryan had exchanged.

"I'm sorry, Miss Quinn. Here." The man produced a piece of paper and pen.

"Thank you." She wrote a fast *To Celia — With Best Wishes! Kayla Quinn.* Handing the paper back to the man, she said, "If you'll give me your address, I'll send your daughter a photo, too."

At his wife's nudging, Edward drew a card from his wallet and gave it to Kayla.

There was an awkward moment when no one said anything. Then the man and woman both began to thank Kayla at the same time, and they all laughed. The couple wished her well in the competition and hurried off in the direction of the restaurant.

Kayla sat for a minute in the quiet darkness of her car. A row of oak trees, stripped of their leaves in preparation for winter, arced over the snow-dusted pavement. Their stark branches shook under the wind's vicious attack; the more fragile limbs snapped and moaned in protest of the cold.

The bleak scene sent a chill through Kayla, and she thought again of New Hampshire and the years she'd spent there in the cozy house of her former coach and his wife. Cleo and Sharon, as she usually called her foster parents, had taken her into their home after her parents' deaths. The couple treated her as if she were their own child — the daughter they'd never been able to have. And she'd grown to love them as much as she'd allowed herself to love anyone since the loss of her mother and father.

Was she thinking of them now because her life all at once seemed assaulted by puzzling uncertainties? If she and Ryan failed to place in the Golden Skates, how could they hope to gain the momentum they'd need to triumph at Worlds in a few short months? Worlds would be their last chance to make a permanent mark as a pair before going their separate ways.

A feeling of emptiness invaded her heart as she put the key in the ignition and set the heater vents on full blast. She wondered if a trip to New Hampshire might be just what she needed.

The last time she'd seen Cleo and Sharon had been at Nationals. They'd treated Ryan and her to dinner in celebration of their victory in the competition. The mood that evening was festive, and she and Ryan had acted almost giddy with happiness. And why not? They'd felt as if they owned the world — or at least a small corner of it.

After they'd finished their dessert, Ryan had walked her to her room. He'd bowed and kissed her hand, declaring that she was the most beautiful woman on the face of the earth. She'd smiled and rolled her eyes, aware that he was teasing her — and that he was between girlfriends at the time. He had a way of flattering her in an almost big-brotherly fashion when he had no other female to indulge.

Kayla was surprised to find a tear slipping down her cheek. *Sentimental fool.* Sentimental or not, she made up her mind that she would phone Cleo and Sharon soon. They'd be coming to Colorado for the competition. Maybe she could fly back home with them for a vacation.

But as she drove past the front of the restaurant, Kayla remembered how her partner had looked standing at the entrance, gazing down at her, his breath caressing her cheek. And for some absurd reason, all she could think about was how far away New Hampshire was from Colorado Springs and Ryan Maxwell.

"Come in for a few minutes, Ryan."

Christy whispered the words in his ear as

her fingers toyed with the back of his neck. She knew which strings to pull to get her way with him. But tonight her feminine wiles weren't working their usual magic on him.

"Sorry." He slowly backed away from her. "I have to go home. I've got to be at the arena at five-thirty sharp tomorrow morning."

"So?" She sidled closer and laid her palm against his jacket. "It's only nine o'clock, I'll make some coffee and we . . ." Her hands crept around his neck again.

"No." Ryan extricated himself from her arms. "No more late hours for a while. Not for a long while."

Christy's eyes widened. "I can't believe you're saying that." She suddenly smiled. "Oh, it's Kayla's silly idea, isn't it?"

Ryan squared his jaw. "Kayla doesn't have silly ideas."

The smile became an unruly pout. "It *is* silly when someone expects her partner to abide by her rules. Just because she wants you there at some unearthly hour . . ."

"I expect myself to be at the arena at the agreed-upon time." He was more than a little perturbed. "Kayla has my greatest respect. I couldn't ask for a more dedicated partner."

"Of course. But why did you go running after her when she left the restaurant in a huff?"

"Kayla didn't leave in a huff." Christy had been needling him all night on the subject, and he'd had enough — though he himself couldn't quite figure out the reason for his pursuit of his partner. Or the reason why a slow burn had begun in his stomach at the idea of Kayla dating Brookings. Even now, thinking about it caused an odd tightening in his gut.

"Okay, Ryan. Have it your way."

The harping tone of Christy's voice grated on his nerves. She put her back to him, and he didn't try to stop her as she jabbed the key in the lock of her door. "Good night, Ryan." She flung the words at him and slammed the door shut.

An appropriate end to a wasted evening, he thought. He walked wearily to the elevator. Christy lived on the eighth floor of the luxury high-rise in the heart of downtown Colorado Springs. The structure appeared to be all glass and cold steel to Ryan. Waiting by the elevator, he realized how much more at home he felt in his plain efficiency on the west side of town, or in Kayla's modest apartment in an older brick building on tree-lined Tejon Street.

When the elevator door slid open, Ryan pushed the button that would take him to the parking garage. He slumped against the carpeted wall of the elevator and buried his hands in his jeans pockets. His fingers closed around the folded piece of paper that he'd stashed in the right pocket. Earlier, outside the Pizza Connection, he'd been tempted for a second to share Eve's "love triangle" with Kayla, thinking it might lighten up her testy mood. Thankfully, his better judgment had prevailed, and he'd seen that it was an asinine idea. Why should he bother Kayla with the coach's crazy notions?

Taking out the wrinkled piece of paper, he stared at the drawing. At the moment, he saw nothing amusing about it himself. There was only one place Eve's artwork belonged. He wadded the piece of paper into a ball in the palm of his hand and held onto it until the elevator rolled to a stop.

A bitter blast of wind greeted him when he stepped outside. Another caught him square in the face as he walked through the maze of parked cars and concrete posts that marked the ground level of the garage.

He recognized Justin's white Audi parked in one of the spaces. While Justin and Christy and a couple of the other skaters had opted for fancier digs in the high-rise after earning a few fat paychecks from exhibitions, Ryan had kept his lifestyle simple. Then, so had Kayla. His one indulgence had been his BMW. Kayla's? He couldn't think of a single thing unless it was that gigantic aquarium she'd bought to house the angelfish he'd given her a few weeks ago.

Money had never been in plentiful supply in his life, and that was one reason, he reminded himself now, that he had to be grateful for the modest financial security a job at Bill's rink would afford him.

Bending his head against the gale, Ryan sprinted to his car. Just as he was about to get in, he spied a trash barrel nearby. He took aim and hurled the wadded piece of paper into the barrel. It danced around the rim a couple of times, then made a perfect landing in the middle of a mound of soda cans and take-out chicken boxes.

"Rest in peace," he said, wishing he could discard his troubles just as easily. But for all his conviction that the coach was misinformed about his relationships and where they were headed, he had to admit that his woes lately seemed to revolve around two women. Kayla and Christy.

What was it anyway that had them so upset with each other — and him? Women. Who could figure them out? It was a sure bet he'd never be able to.

A burst of wind buffeted the car, and Ryan shivered. Time to crank up the engine and head home. There was nothing to be gained by freezing to death while trying to make sense of what was on Kayla's and Christy's minds. He let the car idle for a minute while he thawed his hands.

It occurred to him that he could be up in Christy's apartment at that moment, snuggling with her on the sofa. She'd warm his hands. But what about his heart? The question troubled him, and the idea of holding Christy in his arms suddenly held no appeal. He assumed it was due to the words they'd exchanged.

The truth slammed into him when he closed his eyes, and the burning started again in his insides. Kayla was there, in his mind. It was Kayla he wanted to hold.

His hands started to shake, and he curled them into fists to stop the trembling. Was he nuts? He'd been priding himself on his self-control, and here he was longing after his partner — the one woman who was totally off limits for him.

The shaking eased when he realized that

it wasn't just that he wanted to hold Kayla. He needed to tell her that everything was going to be okay, that they were going to iron out the kinks in their program and win the Golden Skates. He longed to assure her that her future was secure — no matter that his knee was on the skids and he had no clue as to how he was going to hold it together to take the title at Worlds. But he'd do it somehow.

Have to, he thought. *Then Kayla'll have the top touring outfits in the country courting her like crazy.*

Yet common sense told Ryan he couldn't promise her any of those things. So, as he drove off in the dead of an early winter's night, he made a silent vow to her that he knew he could keep.

Tomorrow morning — and every morning for as long as they were partners — he would be at the arena to greet her when she stepped onto the ice.

Chapter Four

"I must be seeing an illusion," Kayla quipped.

Ryan grinned. "Is that any way to greet your partner?"

She couldn't help it. He'd caught her so much by surprise that those were the first words that had popped out of her mouth. He stood at the boards, one leg crossed over the other, his arms folded against his chest, as if it were his usual pattern to be on the ice before the crack of dawn on a winter morning. "Do you know, Ryan, that this is . . ."

". . . the third time in three years that I've beat you to the rink?" He closed the gap between them. "I promise you it won't be the last. I intend to open up the arena every morning from now on."

Who was this changed man standing before her? Kayla wondered. "So you didn't burn the candle at both ends last night?" she teased.

He laughed, but his eyes held a guarded expression. "If you're fishing for when I tucked myself into bed, it was ten o'clock on the nose. I didn't even stay up to watch our interview on the late news."

She'd skipped the news on purpose. Why subject herself again to that silly little reporter flirting her way into Ryan's good graces? But the fact he'd gone to bed at ten meant that he hadn't been out late with Christy. No doubt Christy had been sizzling mad at him. The idea made her smile.

"What's so funny?"

"Oh, nothing."

"Well then, did you get your beauty sleep?"

She shifted her gaze away from him. "As always." In truth, the last time she'd checked the clock, it had been quarter to midnight. After she'd tried to reach Cleo and Sharon and failed, she'd taken a leisurely bath and gone to bed. But while her body had been dead tired, her mind had been wide awake, busy rehashing the confrontation between Ryan and herself outside the Pizza Connection. If she hadn't known better, she'd have said they'd acted more like jealous lovers than friends and partners. Finally, she'd fallen asleep, determined to make a fresh start of things with him in the morning.

"We should both be ready for a hot session, wouldn't you say, Kayla?"

"Yes . . . hot," she agreed, not quite meeting his eyes.

"Just the kind of dedication I love to see in my pupils."

Kayla swung around in surprise. Would she ever get used to the coach sneaking silently up on her like that?

"I thought we'd begin with your short program." Eve beamed at both of them. "Unless one of you has a better idea."

Kayla sighed inwardly. She'd hoped they would concentrate on their long program for a few more days, though she had to concede their short program was their weakness. At Nationals they'd been in third place after the short program and barely squeaked by in the long program for the win. They'd reached deep inside themselves and pulled it off then. She was far less certain of their chances now.

"Nope. No better ideas," Ryan said. "Kayla?"

"No ideas."

"Let's not look glum. At least we won't have the judges breathing fire down our backs," Eve offered. "By the time they file into the stands, you two will be ensconced at Estelle's, knee-high in costumes and kids."

Kayla glanced at her partner. "Be glad for small favors." She grimaced. He smiled good-naturedly. Maybe he'd decided to make a new start, too. After all, he'd shown up early for practice. *Right. As he himself said, for the third time in three years.*

"Okay," Eve was saying. "Twenty minutes for warmup." The coach made a dismissive gesture and charged off.

"Eve must've eaten an extra bowl of her famous Scotch oatmeal," Ryan joked.

Kayla laughed. Eve swore by the cereal that she ordered in ten-pound boxes from a company in Scotland. But Kayla feared she and Ryan were in for a grueling session.

After they'd labored through their stretching exercises and executed some easy jumps and spins, they plunged into their short program. From the first aborted throw double Lutz, their performance unraveled into a full-blown disaster, and any hopes they'd entertained for a "hot" practice were dashed by cold reality.

On their side-by-side sit spins, Kayla didn't realize she was half a rotation ahead of Ryan until Eve shouted from the boards,

"Remember, you're not skating solo, Kayla!"

"Ryan, watch the toe pick," the coach admonished moments later as he was lifting Kayla out of her backward outside death spiral.

When the music ended, Kayla avoided her partner's gaze. But she heard his frustration released in the expulsion of a pent-up breath.

Eve motioned them over to the boards, her face flushed with anger. "If I didn't know better, I'd think you two were the new kids on the block — the ones who'd never skated a short program before. Where's the harmony?" Her voice dropped to a dramatic whisper. "Let's figure out some way to restore it, shall we?"

Kayla stared at her skates. Every nerve in her body felt ready to short-circuit. How in the world were she and Ryan expected to recapture their harmony on the ice when they couldn't agree on why — or how — they had lost it?

"All right." Eve gave each of them a pat on the back. "Let's do it one more time."

They did it a dozen more times. As skaters filtered onto the ice, they simply skated around them. And when the rink became crowded and others had official ice time, they executed their short program without the aid of their music.

By eleven-thirty, when Eve told them to call it quits for the day, Kayla was trembling with exhaustion. Her partner didn't look in much better shape. His face wore a sheen of perspiration. His hair was damp, too, and disheveled, but the thing Kayla seemed to notice most was the intriguing way the dark ringlets clung to the back of his neck and his brow.

In the corridor, just short of the locker rooms, Ryan pulled her aside. "I have an errand to run before lunch," he said, backhanding away beads of sweat from his cheeks. "See you at Estelle's, I guess."

Before Kayla could think of a reply, he strode off. Her frustration mounted. They used to eat lunch together sometimes after morning practice. Why not today? It would have given them the perfect opportunity to hash out their woes, maybe even come up with a viable solution to their problems.

But no. Ryan had more important business to attend to. No doubt his errand involved Christy in some manner.

That woman has him at her beck and call, thought Kayla, quickening her pace as she went on to the women's dressing room.

Kayla was passing through the lobby on her way to lunch when Charlie called her over to his desk. "Hi, Charlie," she said. "How are you?" The droopy cast of his eyes made her think that she wasn't the only one who was losing sleep these days.

"Doing all right, Sunshine. How about you?"

"Okay, thanks. I'll be seeing Shelly in a couple of hours at Estelle's."

"I know." He nodded. "That's why I wanted to talk with you. I have a little favor to ask."

"Sure. What is it?"

"Well, Joan's planning on driving the kids over there today in the van. But to tell you the honest truth, I'm afraid she's hardly up to it." His cheeks reddened. "She's still having problems with the morning sickness."

"I'll be glad to make other arrangements for the kids." Kayla recalled they were getting special permission to leave school for the costume fitting.

Charlie's face relaxed. "Tell you what, Sunshine. Joan'll be disappointed if she has to stay home. But I'd appreciate if you'd watch out for her. If she starts feeling poorly, maybe you and Ryan could give the kids a lift home."

"Don't worry." Kayla offered the guard a reassuring smile. "We'll take good care of the kids — and Joan."

"Thanks, Sunshine." He laughed. "I guess I'm a bit overly protective of my wife. But Joan's wonderful, you know, and I love her."

A sudden lump rose in Kayla's throat. "I'm glad to help, Charlie." She looked away before he could see the mistiness in her eyes. Blinking back the wetness, she wondered why she had gone all to mush because someone had told her that he loved his wife.

Kayla counted heads. There were eleven, if she included Joan and Louie, Estelle's white Maltese, who at the moment was confined in a kennel cage set near the front counter of the seamstress's shop. The kids had nicknamed the tiny dog Loony Louie for his crazy antics whenever he was let loose to roam. Now the animal looked forlorn as he stared up at Kayla through the barred door of the cage.

There was plenty of chaos without Louie. Shelly, Gina, and Jennifer were huddled together, giggling, while Nathan, Petey, Drew, and Micah were engaged in a minor wrestling match. Their exuberance was likely due to their early release from school. At least the members of the club were present and accounted for. Ryan was not.

Joan sat on a chair that Estelle efficiently provided for her. Her plain but pleasant face looked white and drawn to Kayla. With some alarm, Kayla wondered if the expectant mother was about to faint. "Can I get you a glass of water?" she asked, bending over Joan.

"Oh yes, thank you."

Joan offered a wan smile as she took the paper cup from Kayla. "I suppose Charlie told you that he didn't want me to come. I swear, he fusses over me like a mother hen."

"He's just concerned about you, Joan. I want you to know that if at any time you need to leave, Ryan and I will be happy to . . ."

"Stop it, Nathan!" Gina's wail drowned out Kayla's last words.

Kayla straightened, suddenly glad she'd consumed a hearty lunch at the café. It appeared she would need the boost of energy the soup and sandwich had given her. "Okay, what's the problem?"

Gina's lower lip was thrust out, and there was a haughty set to her freckled, heart-shaped face. "Nathan tried to rip the sash off my dress." The girl plucked at the folds of her aqua costume.

Nathan shoved his blond hair back from his eyes and scowled. "No way. I wouldn't *touch* her dress." His nose screwed up in an expression of disgust. "But she was gonna steal my bow tie."

Kayla hid a smile. She suspected that the girl picked fights with the ten-year-old boy because she had a huge crush on him. "Gina, I think the best solution is for you to go over and stand by Joan until Estelle calls for you. Nathan, you can stay with me." She didn't miss the face the boy made at Gina in passing.

"Children, I want the rest of you to line up by the wall." Estelle's authoritative voice seemed to weave a sort of spell as the kids obeyed her without a whimper. With a tape measure hung around her neck and a pincushion that resembled a gigantic strawberry strapped to her wrist, the plump white-haired seamstress exuded an air of calmness. "Shelly, let me have a look at your dress."

Shelly skipped to the center of the room. Her costume of pale yellow chiffon complemented her long chestnut-brown hair. The sight of the little girl pirouetting in front of the seamstress reminded Kayla of one of those porcelain ballerinas that grace the tops of antique music boxes.

In fact, all of the kids' outfits looked just perfect. Ryan had conceived the idea of the boys wearing tuxedos patterned closely after the one he would be wearing in the competition. The girls' dresses were of a similar design to Kayla's, except that theirs were fashioned of chiffon in a rainbow of pastel shades while hers was of white satin material with a lace bodice that sported intricate beadwork. Kayla was still amazed that her partner had managed to persuade the patrons of the local figure skating community to foot the bill for the kids' costumes.

Estelle finished with Shelly and called for Petey to come forward. The boy strolled over to the seamstress, a study in self-consciousness with his hands thrust in the pockets of his tux. At seven, Petey Gomez was the youngest member of the club — and the most enthusiastic of the group when he was on skates. But trying on costumes was apparently not his thing.

"Hold still, Petey, or you're bound to wind up with more holes than a pincushion," the seamstress warned. But the boy frowned and wiggled all the while Estelle was tacking up his pants legs and taking tucks in his waistband.

The woman has the patience of a saint, decided Kayla.

"There," Estelle clucked and shook her head. "That wasn't so bad, was it?"

Petey grinned shyly at the seamstress. "I s'pose not."

"Hmmph. Now you won't be tripping all over your pants during that big production number." With a light tap on Petey's posterior, Estelle sent the boy back to his post and called Drew's name.

Absorbed in watching Estelle at work with the kids, Kayla didn't realize anyone was on the other side of her until she felt a tug on her sleeve. She turned to find Shelly looking expectantly at her. "When are you going to put on your costume?" the girl asked.

"In a few minutes, Shelly. I'm waiting for Ryan to come."

"Is he always late?" Shelly asked with typical childlike directness.

"No. Not always." Kayla put her arm around the girl, hoping her impatience didn't show.

Estelle had just finished with Drew when Ryan strode through the door, his arms loaded with boxes.

All activity ceased for a moment, and even the club members grew quiet. The

81

kids eyed their mentor as he bent to place a kiss on Estelle's cheek. "Sorry I'm late," he said.

Estelle brushed him off with a wave of her hand. "Well, you're here now," she said gruffly. "It's high time you and Kayla were putting on your costumes."

Ryan set the boxes down in a pile near Estelle's feet. "We will, but first I wonder if you'd allow me a couple of minutes to show everyone what I've got here."

Though he was talking to the seamstress, Kayla noticed that he was looking at her.

"I'll bet it's new skates," Gina declared.

"Are they for us?" Petey piped in.

Ryan held up his hand. "Not so fast, Petey. With Estelle's permission, I'll open the boxes."

The seamstress's face softened. "Now how can I refuse when you've got me curious too?"

Kayla watched in fascination as her partner separated the boxes into two piles. Then, with a grin and a flourish, he lifted the lid off one of the boxes. Gasps and giggles and a couple of "oh's" burst forth as Ryan pulled out a small black top hat.

"Wow!" exclaimed Nathan and Drew at once.

"There's a hat just like this one in each of the other three boxes," Ryan said, walking over to place the top hat on Petey's head.

All reticence forgotten, Petey marched directly to the full-length mirror on the other side of the room. He studied his reflection frontways, then sideways, from every angle. He drew the hat forward on his head, then pushed it back until he was satisfied that it fit just right.

Ryan handed the other boys their hats. "And now, for the girls," he said with a wink in Kayla's direction.

Titters erupted again from the girls as he went through the same ritual in pulling off the lid of the first box in the other pile. The titters gave way to gasps when he held up a white shiny headband adorned with a cluster of yellow satin roses. "Mmm." He smiled. "Shelly? I believe this one has your name on it."

"Neat," the girl breathed.

Ryan gave the headband to Estelle, who fitted it over Shelly's hair.

The other girls came forward. Gina's headband sported aqua roses, Jennifer's deep pink.

In that instant, Kayla's admiration for her partner increased immeasurably. He'd obviously bought the hats and headbands out of his own money. And the pieces were custom-made to match the kids' outfits. His gaze locked with hers as he came toward her, and the sounds of laughter and chatter seemed to fade away.

"You heard Estelle's orders," he said. "It's time to suit up." He started to lead the way to the dressing rooms.

Kayla stopped him with a hand on his arm. "You did something very special, Ryan."

He shrugged. "I thought the kids' costumes needed a little extra pizzazz."

It was just like him, Kayla realized, to make light of his deed. But then somehow she'd always known that beneath that headstrong exterior beat the heart of a modest, generous man.

Chapter Five

"Ouch!"

"What happened, Ryan?"

"Nothing, Kayla." Nothing except that his elbow had just collided for the third time with the back wall of the changing booth. *They don't make these places to accommodate a five-foot, eleven-inch man,* he thought, twisting his arms pretzel-fashion in a futile attempt to free himself of his shirt. Finally, after a couple of more tries, the shirt came off.

Kayla was in the next cubbyhole over, changing into her costume.

"Are you ready yet?" she asked.

He pulled on the top, then the pants of the tux outfit. "Almost." He grunted, jerking up the pants.

"I'll go on out," she called back.

Ryan wasn't surprised that she beat him getting dressed. With her petite frame, she would've had no trouble maneuvering around the matchbook-sized room. He finished buttoning and zipping his tux. Emerging from the booth, he made a check of his image in the mirror that hung on the front of the door. The costume appeared to fit fine, but he noticed that his hair was in need of a good combing — and a cut, he decided, running his fingers through it.

The changing booths were located in an alcove at the rear of Estelle's shop. Ryan got as far as the archway of the alcove when the sight of his partner stopped him dead in his tracks. Kayla stood in the center of the room with her back to him. Estelle was kneeling in front of her, doing something to the hem of Kayla's dress. But it wasn't the seamstress's activities that caused the breath to catch in Ryan's throat. It was the costume. Or rather, it was Kayla in the costume.

He noted that she'd taken down her hair from the usual ponytail she sported at practice. It tumbled in dark waves over the lace and white satin material of her costume. The dress fit snugly against Kayla's back, emphasizing the trimness of her waist, the soft, feminine flare of her hips where the skirt fell in folds against her thighs.

"Come over here, Ryan, and let's have a look at you."

It was a second before Estelle's command registered in his mind, and another second before he could get his feet in gear to cross the room. The older woman stood up and regarded him as he headed toward her.

Estelle smiled broadly. "Now don't you look just as handsome as a groom on his way to be married."

Ryan froze in mid-step. *A groom on his way to be married?* Belatedly, he noticed that Kayla was staring at him.

Giggles broke out from the girls in the club. "If Ryan's the groom, then Kayla's the bride," Gina announced.

Ryan shot the girl a stern glance, but Gina was busy smothering another round of the giggles. To his dismay, he saw that Kayla's cheeks were suffused with color. He felt too warm himself, and a little shook up. Kayla did resemble a bride — blushing and beautiful in the stunning dress of white satin. And he was prepared to swear on a stack of trophies that he'd never imagined the two of them would look like a pair hotfooting it to the altar.

He thought of the headband he'd had designed to go with the dress. Its white feathers and satin roses would add a snazzy touch to Kayla's costume, he'd figured. Ironically, he'd come up with the idea in hopes the gift might serve to perk up her flagging spirits.

He had purposely left the headband in the car, with the clever notion of presenting it to her later. Now he wished to heaven that he'd brought the gift along inside instead of planning on making a minor deal out of it by giving it to her privately.

"You're through, dear." Estelle gave Kayla's arm a squeeze. "You can go on."

Kayla didn't move for a moment. Then she seemed to realize that Estelle had spoken to her. "I'll see you, Ryan," she said, passing him without a glance.

"Wait for me," he called after her.

She acted as if she hadn't heard him, but he couldn't stop himself from admiring how her silky costume swirled around her shapely thighs with every retreating step.

"Ryan, goodness, hold your leg still."

Estelle's reprimand cut into his thoughts. "Sorry," he said. He wasn't conscious that he'd been jiggling his leg. The seamstress was on her knees, poking pins into the inseam of his pants, and he recalled his conversation with Eve. "The coach and I discussed adding stripes to the seams of the tux."

Estelle flapped her hand, as if she were shooing away a fly. "Yes, yes, I know all about that. And I told her that the tuxedo should be left alone. She said, 'Whatever you think is best, Estelle.' "

Ryan smiled to himself. Estelle was the only person he knew who always managed to get her way with the coach. He hadn't been that crazy about the stripe idea in the first place.

"Can we play with Loony Louie now?"

Petey's question made Ryan aware that the kids were still standing around. They'd been remarkably well-behaved.

"Not until after you change out of that costume, young man," the seamstress retorted.

"Oh, boy!" Petey made a dash for the alcove.

"Ladies first, Petey."

The youngster turned a look of guileless bewilderment on the seamstress. "But there isn't any ladies here, 'cept Kayla — and she's already changing her clothes."

Ryan concealed another smile as Estelle sighed. "*Aren't* any ladies, Petey," she corrected. "And yes, there are other ladies. Besides Joan and myself, there are Shelly,

Gina, and Jennifer. And since you're a young gentleman, I'm sure you'll be happy to allow the three lovely ladies in costume to use the dressing rooms first."

"Gina's no lady," Nathan asserted. The other boys snickered, and Nathan grinned broadly.

"You're no gentleman, either," Gina dished back, thrusting out her dimpled chin.

Ryan clapped his hands. Apparently the kids had been too well behaved. He should've known it couldn't last. "All right, knock it off. Nathan, Gina, I want you both to apologize." He watched as the two mumbled a mutual "I'm sorry," with their heads hung down. "Ladies, you can go ahead and change first, just as Estelle said. Gentlemen, while you're waiting patiently for your turn, put your hats away in the boxes for safekeeping."

Ryan swapped winks with Estelle. She seemed to be done with whatever adjustments she'd been making in his tux. "There, that should do," she said, accepting the hand he offered her as she rose slowly to her feet. "The costumes should be ready in a week or so." She smoothed the wrinkles from her skirt.

He calculated that would give the club

enough time to stage at least one or two dress rehearsals before the big night. As he went to wait his turn for a booth, he saw that Kayla was back, dressed in her jeans and a red sweater. She was over by Charlie's wife, who'd been sitting off to herself.

Joan had obviously brought the kids today. She looked bushed. Had the afternoon been too much for her to handle, with her pregnancy? Ryan hoped that Kayla would stay occupied with Joan until he was done changing out of the tux.

Kayla was still there when he stepped out of the booth, but Loony Louie was on the loose as well. The Maltese tore past Ryan like a mini white tornado. The kids added to the confusion, shrieking and lunging for the little dog as he streaked around the room.

Ryan went to join Louie's mistress by the counter. From the corner of his eye, he saw Kayla coming his way.

"That dog." Estelle shook her head. "When the children are here, Louie's like a hen on a hot griddle."

"Or maybe a chicken with its head cut off," Ryan said. Kayla smiled up at him, and he found himself staring for a second too long into those lush brown eyes.

Louie charged past the outside of his

kennel, yipping. Then he made a straight shot for Shelly and bounded into the girl's arms, nearly knocking her off her feet. That sent the kids into gales of laughter.

Ryan decided it was time to call it a day. "Okay, club members," he called above the din. "Louie's had enough exercise for now. And Estelle's had enough of us. Let's hit the road and give her back her shop." To the seamstress, he whispered, "And your peace and quiet."

"I have enough of that. You know, I do love children," she added in a sort of wistful voice.

It dawned on Ryan that maybe the older woman was lonely, that she got considerable enjoyment out of having the kids around. "You'll be seeing a lot more of the club members in the months and years to come," he told her. "Kids grow fast, and there'll be a need for a bunch more costume fittings, I'm afraid." The beaming smile on Estelle's face told him he'd said the right thing.

The next instant, Kayla stepped up to him. "Can I talk to you, Ryan?"

"Sure, partner."

Estelle cleared her throat. "If you'll both excuse me . . ."

"I guess she thinks we want to be alone."

Ryan meant it as a joke, but Kayla didn't laugh. "What is it?" He remembered Charlie's wife. "Is Joan okay?"

"Not really. Charlie asked me if you and I could be on standby to chauffeur the kids in case Joan wasn't up to it. She insists she's all right, but she looks very pale."

"I noticed. No problem. We'll drive the kids home."

"You don't have to meet Christy right away?"

"Nope. I won't be seeing her tonight." The truth was, he hadn't seen Christy all day, and he'd thought of asking Kayla to have dinner with him. The two of them used to go off and have lunch or dinner by themselves occasionally. He found he missed her company. Besides, it was early, and he wasn't ready to go home to an empty apartment yet.

"Tell Joan not to worry," he said, "just take good care of herself." He hesitated, then added, "Ask Estelle to stall the kids for a few minutes, which should be a piece of cake for her. Then meet me outside in the parking lot, I have a surprise for you."

"A surprise for me?"

Her puzzlement made him chuckle. "Just go on."

Moments later, he was reaching inside

his car for the box he'd stashed on the back seat. He placed it in Kayla's hands. She stared at the box, then at him, "Open it," he urged.

Kayla removed the lid and peered inside. "Oh, how lovely." She lifted out the headband and ran her fingers over the feathers and flowers. "I assume you bought a top hat for yourself."

"Sure did." He took the headband from her hands and fitted it gently over her hair. Then she turned to look at herself in the car window.

"It's perfect," she declared, touching a feather.

"I agree." He smiled at her reflection.

"Thank you, Ryan."

Before he knew what was happening, Kayla was hugging him. His arms automatically closed around her. "You're welcome," he said against her hair. His nose picked up the lavender smell of her soap or cologne. The scent was nice — not overpowering like the stuff that Christy wore, but fresh and natural like Kayla herself. Funny he'd never paid attention to the fragrance until now.

She tilted her head and gazed into his face. Then she brought her lips to his. Too late he realized that she'd only meant to plant a chaste kiss on his cheek. But he'd moved a fraction, and their mouths met.

That was all it took. The incredible softness of her lips against his caused all common sense to flee, and he captured her mouth in a real kiss. Her lips were like velvet, the taste of her far sweeter than he could ever have imagined. A now-familiar tightening spread through his insides, an unquenchable thirst that compelled him to hold her possessively as she returned his kiss.

Suddenly she stiffened in his arms, and he felt her beginning to withdraw. That snapped him to his senses. He jerked away as if he'd been touching a hot stove and was in imminent danger of suffering third-degree burns. He'd been playing with fire all right — the kind that had already left his heart scarred for life.

An image of Gillian wheeled through his mind. He saw again the look of confusion darkening her eyes that evening in her apartment when he'd let her know his interest in her went beyond platonic friendship. He saw the same expression now in Kayla's eyes, and a sick feeling hit him like a punch in the stomach. Yet the sight of her moist, parted lips made the flames leap higher, tempting him to kiss her again, to throw caution to the devil and pull her flush against his body until there wasn't any room for doubt between them.

He dropped his gaze and clenched his hands at his sides to keep them from encircling her waist. Silently cursing himself, he tried to muster an apology. The words got stuck in his throat when he glanced at his partner.

Her face was turned from him. "Tell Gina and Nathan and Jennifer that I'm waiting for them," she said. Her voice sounded hollow, like a distant echo.

Ryan opened his mouth. Still, nothing came out. He reached to touch her, then quickly withdrew his hand. "I'll tell them," he said at last.

He waited for a long heartbeat, hoping that Kayla would look at him, say something — anything that would tell him things were going to be okay between them. But she was already walking toward her car, and he had no choice except to go back into the shop.

"It was only a kiss." Kayla muttered the words to herself as she drove west on Pikes Peak Avenue. Her charges — Jennifer, Gina, and Nathan — had been safely delivered to their respective parents, and she was on her way home to her apartment.

For the past hour and a half the kids had provided a noisy diversion, and she'd been kept busy negotiating her way through heavy traffic. Now she found herself dwelling on that moment when Ryan's mouth had so smoothly possessed hers.

She told herself that he'd taken advantage of an opportunity that had been presented to him — plain and simple.

But there'd been nothing plain — or simple — about her response to the delicious sensation of his lips moving against hers. For one wild moment all rational thought had escaped her mind, and it had seemed as if she'd been waiting a lifetime for the velvet warmth of his kiss.

Her hands curved tightly around the steering wheel. How in the span of a few seconds could she have left her guard down so completely? There was only one solution. She would have to erase that kiss from her memory. No doubt Ryan had already forgotten it — though the wounded look in his eyes when they'd parted gave her added reason for regretting their mutual lapse in sound judgment.

No doubt he'd find solace tonight in Christy's arms, as Kayla assumed he'd found in the arms of the numerous other beautiful women he'd dated over the years. Was he destined to flit from gorgeous blond to redhead to brunette for the rest of his life, she wondered, seeking a good time and nothing more because he'd vowed never to leave himself open to being hurt again? Or did his determination only apply to his skating partner?

An undeniable stab of jealousy coursed through her at the thought of Ryan's mouth capturing Christy Michaels's in a soulful kiss.

Stop acting like a dizzy teenager, she told herself. She and Ryan were partners and friends — and one kiss was not going to change that fact. Nor did it make a jot of a difference as to their future plans.

At the next intersection the stoplight flashed from yellow to red. Just in time, Kayla hit the brakes, and the Neon swerved to a halt. While she waited for the light to change to green, she glanced at her image in the vanity mirror. Her makeup was worn off, and her hair was full of tangles. Was that what Ryan had seen when he'd made his passion play? Kayla laughed out loud. She hardly looked like an object of desire.

Traffic on Cascade slowed to a crawl; afternoon rush hour in the city was in full swing. At last, Kayla pulled into her reserved space in the parking lot of her building. With Ryan's gift tucked under her arm, she stopped in the lobby to check her mail. There was one envelope in the box. Turning it over, she saw that it was from Cleo and Sharon.

She tore open the envelope and unfolded the one-page letter that was tucked inside. Another smaller piece of paper fell out. Kayla grabbed it before it floated to the floor. She shook her head when she saw that it was a check from her folks. No matter how many times she assured them that she was doing fine, they persisted in sending her "a little something to help her with expenses."

Kayla put the check in her jeans pocket and read the letter while she waited for the elevator. *As you've probably guessed from the postmark,* the letter began, *your father and I are in Toronto.* Kayla examined the envelope. In her haste, she'd overlooked the Canadian postmark.

Cleo was called away on short notice to fill in for Larry Humes in the junior men's competition in the Ice Games, Kayla read on. *You might remember that Larry hasn't been well. Last week he had heart bypass surgery.*

Kayla pictured the burly, good-humored man who had coached alongside Cleo for a number of years before taking a position with a skating club in Boston.

What this means, honey, is that we won't be able to come out for the Golden Skates. Our love and prayers are with you and Ryan, as always. Use the enclosed gift to buy yourself something nice to wear to the annual dinner party. The letter was signed, *All our love, Mom and Dad.*

Disappointment constricted Kayla's heart as she rode the elevator to her floor. She let herself into her apartment, laid the box on the dining table, and sagged onto the sofa with the letter still in her hands.

She understood that Cleo had to help out his friend. But this would be the first year that her folks wouldn't make it to the Golden Skates. After the loss of her parents, Cleo and Sharon's involvement in her career had taken on an added dimension of importance. Their unflagging support was particularly precious to her, and she'd looked forward to the comfort of knowing they would be in the stands at the Golden Skates, cheering her on. Now they weren't coming.

Kayla sat for a long while, staring numbly into space. When her stomach gave a soft growl, she went to the kitchen and fixed herself a cup of tea and a sandwich that she had no appetite for. On passing the aquarium, she realized that she hadn't fed Angelfish Eve since early morning.

The delicate little fish had been a gift from Ryan, too. Watching Angelfish Eve devour the brine shrimp she dumped into the tank, Kayla recalled how Ryan had laughed when he'd learned she was naming the fish after their coach because her fins were like Eve's hands — always in motion.

She thought guiltily of the sweater she'd started knitting for Ryan months ago. It seemed her enthusiasm for finishing the sweater had waned in proportion to her troubles on the ice. Maybe it was time to tackle the project again.

After eating her sandwich, she crossed into the bedroom and opened the drawer where she kept her knitting supplies. Beneath the yarn lay a stack of publicity photos, and she remembered her promise to the couple outside the Pizza Connection.

She tossed the yarn and needles onto the bed and picked a photo from the pile. The black-and-white glossy had been taken right after Nationals. She and Ryan were dressed in their costumes, and they had their arms around each other. Their faces wore radiant smiles. *We were so happy then,* she thought, *ecstatic that we'd won.* Nationals suddenly seemed an eternity ago.

Kayla laid the photo aside. In the morning, she would find an envelope and mail the picture to Celia.

As she was taking off her jeans, she found the check she'd stuffed in the front pocket. Her folks wanted her to buy a new dress to wear to the annual dinner party. But she couldn't care less about new clothes. Nor had she given much consideration to the party, though it was just a week and a half away and was touted as the social affair of the season by the patrons who sponsored the event. She and Ryan had always attended together in the past. But wasn't it a foregone conclusion that he'd be escorting Christy this year?

With an impatient toss, she sent her jeans to the bottom of the empty wash basket. She yanked her rattiest flannel nightgown from the dresser drawer and pulled it over her head. It was the gown she kept in reserve for whenever she was nursing a cold or felt in need of comfort.

For a moment she regarded the rich

maroon-colored yarn spread out on her bed. If she worked diligently, she might be able to complete the sweater in time to give it to Ryan as a parting gift.

A parting gift. The words resounded through Kayla's mind, chilling her with their sense of finality.

She snatched up the yarn and needles and settled herself on the sofa, where she set furiously to knitting. She didn't quit until her fingers ached to the bone. Examining her project, she was pleased to count eleven completed rows. But she could have wept when she saw that she had dropped stitches in almost every one of those rows. All her hard work that evening was for nothing.

Chapter Six

Ryan leaned against the boards, impatient for Petey to arrive for practice. It was Saturday morning, and he was dog-tired. Eve had just put him and his partner through three torturous days of practice on their short program, and he wasn't sure the efforts had paid off. They had maybe marginally improved the program, but their jumps and spins weren't up to snuff, to the level of competency they normally demanded of themselves.

The fact that he hadn't been sleeping well was sure to be affecting his performance on the ice. True, he had been as good as his word and had quit the partying with Christy. But there was something far more urgent on his mind, threatening his powers of concentration. And that was his relationship with Kayla.

He should have known better than to kiss her. He *did* know better. But for the first time in their relationship, he'd let passion get the mastery over his power of reason. Now he had to live with the feelings of regret that hounded him — and do battle with his mounting desire to sweep her into his arms and take possession of her lips again.

"Ryan! Watch this."

Petey's voice sliced into Ryan's thoughts, and he looked up just in time to see the small boy charging toward him over the ice.

"Whoa, Petey! Slow down."

Ryan's admonition came too late as Petey's legs flew out from under him. He landed on his rear and slid to a stop inches from Ryan's feet.

Ryan offered Petey a hand. "You okay, pal?"

The boy looked as if his pride had taken a worse beating than his body. "I'm okay," he muttered. Springing to his feet, he vigorously set about brushing the ice chips from his pants.

Ryan put himself on eye level with Petey. "Were you going to show me your toe loop?"

A tentative smile lit up Petey's face. "Uh-huh," he said.

"Tell you what. Why don't you spend a little time warming up first. Make two, three rounds of the ice. Then you can try the toe." Ryan sent the boy off, wishing he felt more enthusiasm for the practice session ahead.

"Good morning, Ryan."

His muscles tightened involuntarily as he faced his partner. "I didn't know you were there." His gaze touched on hers, then he looked away.

"I just got here," she said.

Kayla sounded like she was tired too — and edgy, he noticed. He finally glanced at her. She was staring out over the rink, and he followed her lead. The Zamboni had smoothed the ice earlier; the surface looked as shiny as blue-white silk, just the way he liked it. He also liked the relative calm that prevailed at the arena on a weekend morning. Ironically, it was when he and Kayla were acting as coaches instead of partners that he'd found their relationship seemed less tense, more natural, the way it used to be. But that was before the kiss.

He spied Scott and Meghan at the other end of the rink. The pair were supervising Drew and Gina as the two youngsters rehearsed their parts for the production number.

"It's great to see the kids so enthused,"

he offered as a way to break the silence. Stealing another glance at Kayla, he saw that she looked stone serious.

"Yes," was all she said.

"Enthusiasm's good for everyone's morale, Kayla." He was rewarded when she made a half turn toward him. "Watch," he said. "Petey's going to perform for us."

The young boy was in position for the toe loop. His right arm and shoulder were back, his left arm and shoulder directed forward. He went into a counterclockwise rotation, then launched himself into the air. "Arms in, Petey! Tight to the chest now," Ryan called out.

The boy executed one revolution in the air and came down — too soon. He wobbled, but managed to stay on his feet. Ryan waved him over to the boards. "That was a good effort," he said. He caught a whiff of Kayla's cologne as he grasped the boy by the shoulders — and nearly lost his train of thought. "Let me show you something, Petey." He turned the boy away so that he was facing in the other direction.

"Okay. When you lift off, you want to remember to bring your arms in close. Pretend you're scooping Loony Louie up in your arms." The boy responded with a giggle. "That way you'll go higher in the air, and your feet won't wobble when you come down. Got it, pal?"

Petey gave a confident nod. "Got it."

"Give it a few practice runs. Then come let me see the toe again."

"You have such wonderful rapport with Petey."

Kayla's quiet comment drew Ryan's immediate attention.

"It's easy for me to feel a kinship to him," Ryan said with a slight smile. "He reminds me of myself when I was his age. That is, the kid appears to have more heart than talent for the sport of figure skating. But he may surprise us all."

"I think he will. But I don't believe the part about you lacking talent."

Ryan couldn't keep his gaze from roving over his partner. She wore a pink warm-up suit that nicely emphasized her curves. "That's because I was a late bloomer." He hoped to win a smile from her, but she looked into the stands.

"I imagine you're getting anxious to begin coaching in earnest," she said.

His heart gave a hard slam in his chest. "I sure am," he said, cursing himself for telling her a lie.

All he needed, he told himself, was a little time — and a ton of willpower — to get mastery over his emotions. Kayla was uptight, too. The competition was looming in front of them. Worlds was around the corner. Once they achieved their goals, they'd be able to shake down, go their own ways, pursue their individual careers. That's how it would be, had to be. *Won't it?* he asked himself.

"You know, Kayla," he said, "you should be giving serious thought to signing on with an agent."

She rounded on him. "You think I'm not aware of that?" she retorted.

He crossed his arms over his chest. "But you haven't done anything about it yet, have you?"

She greeted his question with a chilly silence. *Why am I pressing her?* he wondered. Yet he couldn't seem to give it up. "Bill has a number of contacts in the business," he went on. "He'd be more than glad to help you out." It dawned on Ryan that what he really wanted to do was tell her to stay away from Brookings. But if he did, she might be stubborn enough to go straight to the agent and sign on with him. Besides, she might still be dating Brookings. And that notion bugged Ryan a whole lot more than he cared to admit.

"I have to go," Kayla said suddenly.

"Shelly just came in."

"Huh?" By the time her words registered in Ryan's mind, she was gone. He was tempted to skate after her — for what purpose he hadn't a clue. He made himself stay put. Shelly was here for her lesson. Petey was coming back to show off his jump. It was going to be a long morning.

"Shelly's doing real well, isn't she?"

Kayla observed Charlie's eager face. Beside him, Joan looked less anxious than her husband — and considerably less pale than she had earlier in the week at Estelle's. "She's making wonderful progress," Kayla said. "She's already adept at both the flip and the Salchow. I told her this morning that we'd include the Salchow in her solo debut during the production number." Ryan had skillfully choreographed the number, giving each of the club members a minute alone in the limelight to show off the jumps and spins that they'd mastered.

"That's terrific, Sunshine." Charlie beamed from ear to ear as he put his arm around his wife.

Kayla darted a glance toward the exit near where she stood. She was watching for Shelly to return from the dressing room. But she also had her eye out for any sign of

Ryan. He'd made a beeline for the lockers right after practice was finished, without so much as a wave in her direction.

She wasn't quite sure why she was so anxious to see him when she'd been the one who'd left him cooling his heels the past few days after their practice sessions. Maybe it was because she still hadn't told him the news that her folks wouldn't be coming to the Golden Skates.

"Here's our girl now," Charlie said.

Shelly was headed their way, her knapsack flung over her shoulder. "If you'll excuse me, Charlie . . . Joan," Kayla said, "I need to find someone."

She started down the corridor with the thought of running into Ryan. But the hallway was empty, and there was none of the usual loud talk and raucous laughter drifting from the men's locker room. A feeling of disappointment circled Kayla's heart. She suspected that her partner had beat a hasty exit from the arena.

On her way back from the women's dressing room, she caught up with Meghan.

"I assumed you'd left," her friend said as Kayla fell into step beside her.

"I'm leaving now. You haven't seen Ryan, have you?"

"A few minutes ago. Christy was waiting for him outside the men's locker."

"No doubt they have a date."

"If they do, Ryan didn't seem thrilled about it."

"Really?"

"He never looks happy when he's with Christy. Don't tell me you haven't noticed," Meghan said with a grin. "So have you bought a new dress for the party?"

"No." Kayla slowed her steps. "Cleo and Sharon sent me a check as usual, said I should buy something nice to wear. I'm not sure I will, though. I'm not much in a party mood." *For reasons I'd rather not go into.* Aloud, she said, "My folks won't be coming to the Golden Skates."

"Why? They always come to watch you and Ryan skate."

"I know, but there was an emergency." Increasing her pace again, Kayla explained about Larry Humes's surgery.

"Have you told Ryan?"

"Not yet."

"You'd better. He'll sure be disappointed. Do you two have your plans all set for the party?"

"I . . . don't think we'll be going together this year."

"What?" Meghan's eyes widened. "I

can't believe he hasn't said anything about it."

"I can. Isn't it a given that he'll be taking Christy? Which is fine with me," Kayla added, a shade too defensively.

"I don't believe that, Kayla. He'll want to go with you."

Kayla wondered why her friend was so certain of what Ryan Maxwell wanted to do and not do. "He has less than a week to make up his mind. Actually, I'm thinking of going alone this year." Where that notion had come from, she hadn't a clue. "Or I might invite Hamil Brookings."

"Hmm. The agent with eight arms — that is, if Christy is to be believed."

Kayla rolled her eyes. "An undeserved reputation," she corrected. She wasn't going to confess that one date with the man hardly qualified her as an expert on his honor. When she cast a glance at Meghan, she saw that her friend was smiling.

"Well, whether Hamil Brookings is lecherous or not, let's go shopping this afternoon. We can hit the mall stores first. If nothing suits our fancy there, we'll try Bingman's and the Dusty Rose Boutique."

They were nearing Kayla's car. "I'm sorry, Meghan, but I'm just not in the mood for shopping today. Maybe to-morrow or Monday."

"You do have it bad, don't you?"

"What are you talking about?"

But Meghan was already walking on to her car. "I'll call you," she said over her shoulder, and Kayla was left to stare in exasperation after her friend.

"It's like I never get to see you."

Ryan regarded Christy over his cup of coffee. Those lips that he'd once thought looked so kissable were fixed in an unattractive frown. "I told you that partying late is out for me," he said. "Practice has to come first — at least for now."

She turned her baby blues on him. "Well, doesn't it for all of us?"

No, not for everyone, he was tempted to tell her. He hadn't counted on her company today, had planned instead to go get a haircut, then catch up on some laundry that had been accumulating in a pile that threatened to reach Pikes Peak proportions. But she had intercepted him outside the men's locker and somehow managed to finagle him into having lunch with her at the café.

"I have to get going," he said. He made a show of checking his watch.

"Not until you see the dress I bought to wear to the dinner party next Friday. It's in my car. You'll love it," she purred, leaning toward him. "It's . . ."

He heard no more. His mind was too busy processing what she'd said before that. The dinner party was next Friday. He should have thought of the event that was held two weeks before the competition. How could it have sneaked up on him so fast? Now Christy was talking about a dress that he was going to love.

"Come on, Ryan." She tugged at his arm.

He started to get up from the booth, then stopped. "Not so fast, Christy."

She regarded him curiously. "What?"

"Sit back down."

She sat, her lips curled in a pout. "Don't tell me, Ryan Maxwell, that you're sticking to your rigid schedule on party night, too."

He took a gulp from his cup. The coffee was tepid and bitter-tasting. "Not a schedule. It's just . . ." He blew out a breath. This wasn't the way he'd imagined things would turn out. "Kayla and I will be attending the party — together."

Christy's eyes narrowed dangerously. "You and Kayla?"

Ryan squared his jaw. "That's what I

said." If Christy hadn't looked so blazing angry, he might have laughed at the absurdity of the situation. He'd never meant to ask Christy to be his date. He and Kayla always went together, and he had no intention of breaking with tradition. Especially not this year. His hands curved tightly around his coffee cup. *But what if Kayla turns me down?* It was a real possibility, given the strained state of their relationship. He tried to shut out the idea, telling himself that it wasn't going to happen.

"I should have known," Christy said. She gave a harsh little laugh. "Well, Ryan . . ." She held her hands in front of her and examined her nails in what seemed to be minute detail. "I can see where your loyalties lie." Her gaze was as cold as rain in winter. "If you go through with your plans, then you can forget having me in your life — for keeps."

He swallowed hard and searched for a response. But Christy sprang up from the booth and was gone before he could say a word.

Ryan sat alone, holding the lukewarm cup of coffee for a time as he mulled over the odd twists his life had taken recently. The strange part was, he didn't feel any real regret that his relationship with

Christy was apparently over. He did regret that she'd assumed she'd be his date come next Friday because he hadn't informed her otherwise.

Finally, he rose and went to pay the bill at the register. He'd wasted enough of the day; half of the afternoon was shot already. But the haircut and his laundry would have to wait, just the same. He had something more important that demanded his attention first.

"Hamil here. Sorry I can't answer your call, but if you'll leave your name and your phone number, I'll get back to you soon."

Kayla held the receiver away from her ear. She hadn't considered what she would say if she got the agent's answering machine. But she should have realized that it would be hard to reach him at home. After a moment she hung up. *Don't be silly,* she chided herself. *Just say who you are and ask him to call you.*

She picked up the receiver and dialed again. This time, when the agent's rich baritone voice came on, she left a message. She had just placed the receiver back in its cradle when there was a knock at her door.

Kayla opened the door to find Ryan standing on the other side. Her heart gave

a lurch. "Come in," she said after a second's hesitation.

He looked around expectantly, then took a step into her living room. "Am I interrupting something important?"

"Not a thing," she said, though a minute ago his apology would have been warranted.

There was an awkward moment of silence, then "How's Angelfish Eve?" he asked.

"All right."

The silence stretched between them. "It's been one heck of a week, hasn't it?" he offered.

"Yes . . . it has." *What's the matter with us? Can't we have a normal conversation anymore?* "I got a letter from my folks a few days ago."

"How are they?" he asked, looking away from her.

"Fine." She touched his sleeve. "Oh, Ryan, they won't be here for the competition." The words came out in a rush.

He turned. His eyes searched hers. "Why not?"

"Cleo has to substitute for Larry Humes in the Ice Games. Larry had open-heart surgery." Her gaze went to Ryan's hands. He had them clasped tightly together. She thought of the strength, the warmth in those hands, the way they had drawn her near while his lips moved seductively over hers. "They sent us their love and prayers," she said.

"We can always use those. Kayla . . ."

She raised her eyes. "What?"

"I came to ask . . . will you be my date for the dinner party next week?"

Surely she hadn't heard him correctly. "But aren't you taking Christy?"

"No." He walked over to the window and gazed out. "Christy and I won't be seeing each other anymore."

Now her ears were deceiving her. "You won't be seeing each other?"

"That's right." He made a quarter turn in her direction. "What do you say, Kayla?"

She studied his clean profile, the firm set of his jaw. "I . . . Yes, all right, we can go together." That quickly, she had committed herself.

"I'm sure Eve'll be pleased to hear we're going as a team."

That was it. She understood. Attending the party together wasn't any more a real date this year than it had been in the past. *And why should it be?* she asked herself. *Just because we shared one passionate kiss* . . . "It wouldn't be smart to break with tradition, would it?" she said with a touch of sarcasm.

Ryan didn't answer, only paced from the window to the aquarium. He was walking a little stiffly, favoring his right leg.

"About what happened at Estelle's," he said, staring into the tank.

"Please, Ryan . . ." Kayla took a step toward him.

He raked his fingers through his hair. "I lost my head for a second. That was all."

A lump rose in her throat. She swallowed hard. "We both did," she said.

He faced her. "It won't happen again."

The way his gaze lingered on her mouth, she could have sworn that he meant for it to happen again in the next instant. "No," she said, "absolutely never again."

"Truce then?"

"Truce, Ryan." She averted her eyes as he brushed past her to the door. After he was gone, she sank onto the sofa. She tried to summon positive thoughts about the competition, of Worlds, and of how badly she wanted the wins under her belt so that she could land a juicy contract with the best touring company in the country. But Ryan's presence seemed to fill the room. She snapped off the lamp and shut her eyes. Ryan was still there, breathtaking in his manliness, his black hair glistening in the moonlight as he pulled her into a desperate embrace and covered her mouth and neck with his heady, demanding kisses.

"Eve Baker, please come to the box office," a man's voice boomed over the arena P.A. system. "You have a telephone call."

Kayla stole a questioning look at Ryan. It was four o'clock Wednesday afternoon, and they were in the middle of a marathon practice session that had begun right after lunch. "What do you suppose that's about?" she said, glancing toward Eve, who was standing at the boards with a perplexed expression on her face.

Ryan shrugged. "Hard to tell. Let's find out."

The coach waved them back. "Go on," she called. "I won't be long."

"I guess that means practice, Ryan." Kayla noted that her partner looked exhausted, and she felt more than ready for a hot shower herself.

Two days before, she'd been briefly encouraged when they'd had a productive practice session. They'd teased each other; they'd laughed. Just like old times — almost. She'd begun to think that there was a light at the end of their tunnel of troubles. And she'd credited at least part of her newly optimistic outlook to the fact that she'd given herself a severe talking-to about her relationship with Ryan and her goals for the future. There was no place in her life for thoughts of passionate moonlight encounters with her partner. There was only room for the passion of skating, for seizing the title in the Golden Skates and at Worlds, then landing the contract of her dreams.

But that was before the afternoon's disastrous practice session. A series of missed jumps and stupid mistakes had left her and her partner looking like rank beginners. Further, she sensed that Ryan was holding back whenever they took the ice, playing it too conservatively as they executed their program. Was she holding back, too?

"Kayla?"

She noted that he was avoiding eye contact with her. "I'm ready whenever you are," she said wearily.

They skated past Mitchell and Scott, who were practicing their short programs, and left a wide berth for Fletcher, who was notorious for hogging the ice and sending other skaters scrambling for a toehold as he zoomed by.

But before they could even begin their program, Kayla caught sight of Eve from the corner of her eye. The coach was signaling for them to come to the boards.

An alarm sounded in Kayla's mind the moment she got a good glimpse of Eve. The coach looked as if all the blood had been drained from her face. "Ryan, something's wrong," she said.

"Yeah," he said. His fingers tightened around hers.

They skated up to Eve and flanked her on either side. "Are you okay?" Ryan asked the coach.

"No . . . I'm not." Her hands were unnaturally still.

Kayla put her arm around Eve at the same time that Ryan linked his arm behind the coach's waist. Their fingers met briefly in the middle of Eve's back. "Is it Lila?" she guessed. Lila was Eve's sister, her only close living relative.

"It's Carl," the coach said. "He fell off his tractor. He's in the hospital in Portland . . . in intensive care." Eve's voice sounded faint, far away.

"I'm so sorry." Kayla knew how very fond Eve was of her sister's husband.

"Lila needs me. I'm going to have to go to Portland."

"Yes, of course," Kayla assured her.

"Either of us would do the same," Ryan added. He placed a kiss on Eve's cheek. "Don't worry about us," he said.

Eve offered a shaky smile. "I'm confident that you'll keep practicing diligently in my absence."

"Morning, noon, and night," Ryan promised.

Kayla caught a glimmer of tears in Eve's eyes. Eve blinked them back; she didn't show her emotions easily.

The coach drew her students closer. "I'll book a flight in the morning." She let out a shaky sigh. "You realize I'll be missing the annual dinner party. But I promise I will be back for the competition."

"Stay as long as Lila and Carl need you," Kayla told her.

"You know the shindig won't be the same without you," Ryan said, "even if Kayla and I will be teaming as usual."

Kayla saw the look that passed between her partner and the coach. She had the feeling that the two were exchanging some sort of private message. Then Eve turned to her.

"I do love you both," she whispered in Kayla's ear before skating off.

For a moment Kayla didn't move. Neither, she saw, did Ryan, and it struck her that without Eve to bridge the gap between them, they were standing together yet awkwardly alone.

Chapter Seven

The first thing Kayla did on Friday morning after eating breakfast was to sit down at her desk and begin to compile a list of questions she wanted to ask prospective agents.

The day before, she and Ryan had seen Eve off at the airport amid squalls of snow and a biting wind. As the two of them hugged their coach and sent their best wishes for her brother-in-law's recovery, Kayla hadn't been able to shake the thought that soon they would all be saying farewell to each other — for good. Eve would be staying in Colorado Springs, of course. Ryan would be off to Winding River. *And what about me?* she'd asked herself. *Where will I be headed?*

For a moment, she'd been overtaken by feelings of uncertainty and an almost embarrassing sadness, and she'd had to turn away from Ryan so that he wouldn't see her confusion. Riding beside him in silence on the way back to the arena, she made the decision that it was time to set to work in earnest on the task of finding an agent to represent her interests and help her negotiate a viable contract.

But as she nibbled on a piece of jam-laden toast and sipped on a cup of coffee, she found it increasingly difficult to formulate the questions that she knew she'd need to ask a prospective agent. Her attention was divided, and no matter how hard she tried to focus on the task at hand, her mind kept wandering to thoughts of her partner and the disconcerting effect his presence was having on her lately.

An odd little flutter seemed to take up residence in her stomach whenever she was with him these days. Then there was the rush of warmth that swept over her like a hot wind in July if she allowed herself to dwell on the idea of being in his company for an entire evening at the dinner party.

When she discovered that she'd written the same question twice on the nearly blank piece of paper, Kayla tossed her pen aside and got up from the desk. *It's just a case of nerves,* she told herself as she carried her coffee cup and empty plate through to the kitchen.

With Eve gone, she and Ryan would have to shoulder full responsibility for mingling with the judges at the party — something she didn't look forward to. Unlike her coach and her partner, Kayla wasn't particularly adept at bantering and making small talk with those who held her fate in their hands.

No matter, she thought, *the evening will pass and I'll survive.* But she couldn't so easily dismiss the quiver of excitement that suddenly raced up her spine at the notion that in a matter of hours she would be on Ryan's arm, sweeping up the wide steps of Timberfrost Lodge against a background of twilight skies and snow-draped peaks.

"What'll it be, bud? Sweeney's or the Miner's?"

"Huh? You mean breakfast?" Ryan's thoughts jolted back to the present. He glanced over at Scott, who was jogging alongside him. They'd started their morning with a run, meeting at the corner of Colorado Avenue and 21st Street, just as they used to do on weekends before his knee had started giving him extra grief. But this morning, he'd made up his mind that he needed the run and so he'd wrapped up the knee in a good support bandage and headed out. He was glad that he'd come. The sky was as blue as a bell, and the air had a nice crispness that invigorated him.

"Well?" Scott prompted.

They were nearing the outskirts of Manitou Springs, an artsy village nestled just west of the city at the foot of Pikes Peak. "The Miner's," Ryan decided. The café, located in the heart of the village, served flapjacks the size of dinner plates.

Scott gave a thumbs-up sign, and they finished their run in companionable silence.

As usual, the Miner's was packed, but a booth soon opened up in the rear of the restaurant. The hostess led Ryan and Scott to the table and plunked a menu and a glass of water in front of each of them.

Though he'd been looking forward to sitting down to a meal with his friend, Ryan wondered now if he was up to a gargantuan serving of pancakes. Exercise usually left him plenty hungry, but the past couple of days he hadn't cared if he ate or not. He'd tried to place the blame for his diminished appetite on precompetition worries over whether he and Kayla would finally get it together and pull off a decent enough performance to win the title.

Who am I kidding? he asked himself. With every tick of the clock, the dinner party was drawing closer, and he knew that his anxiety was due to the fact that he was looking forward to escorting Kayla to the party a heck of a lot more than he wanted to acknowledge.

"From what I hear, you and Kayla'll be a twosome tonight." Scott tossed out the statement as if he'd read Ryan's mind.

"Sure, it's a tradition, you know," Ryan said with studied casualness.

Scott chuckled. "Smart to let everyone see that you're tight as a team off the ice, too."

Ryan feigned concentration on the menu. "That's the strategy," he confirmed. Looking up, he saw that his buddy was watching him. "You and Meghan going early for the buffet?"

"Not this year. I'm taking her out to dinner at Sunstone."

"Sunstone." The restaurant was definitely upscale. Ryan had been there a few times with Christy. "Sounds like you're making the evening a special occasion."

"Very special. I plan to ask Meggy to marry me."

Ryan wasn't certain he'd heard right. When he realized that he had, all he could get out was a choked, "Marry you?" before he took a fast gulp of his water.

"Hey, what's so unusual about asking the woman you're in love with to be your wife?"

Ryan offered a shaky smile. "Nothing at all." He extended his hand across the table, and Scott enveloped it in a hearty clasp. "That's great news, I'm really happy for you." He was glad for his friend. So why did the idea of Scott and Meghan getting hitched leave him feeling so uneasy? Had he suddenly gone cold and clammy because he'd pictured his buddy as leading the single life for a good healthy long while — like himself?

"Don't say anything to Kayla, I'm sure Meggy'll want to be the first to break the news. She said she's planning on asking Kayla to be her maid of honor." Scott leveled his gaze at Ryan. "I'd like for you to be my best man."

She's planning on asking Kayla to be her maid of honor. . . . "I'd be pleased to be your best man." Ryan was sincere. But a vision of himself and Kayla standing on either side of the intended bride and groom added a strange new dimension to his already mixed-up feelings — wariness.

"Glad to hear that, bud."

The waitress came by to take their orders. Scott chose the Miner's Special — a plowman's-size meal that included three eggs, three strips of bacon, home fried potatoes, and two pancakes. There was obviously nothing wrong with his appetite.

Ignoring the inquisitive glance Scott telegraphed his way, Ryan opted for the short stack of pancakes. But with his stomach drawn into knots, he wasn't sure if he could do even one of the flapjacks justice.

Unable to bear the idea of sitting around her apartment waiting for the day to pass, Kayla started out on an almost frenzied round of errands, the idea of compiling a list of questions to ask prospective agents all but forgotten. Her first stop was the cleaners to pick up her winter coat. She reasoned that she would need it coming home from the party. Temperatures in the mountains were apt to be frigid that time of year.

After the cleaners, she dropped by a small specialty market to purchase two packages of the hazelnut-flavored coffee that she loved, along with a half dozen of the huge cinnamon rolls that were made fresh on the premises. Detouring to the mall, she window-shopped for a while before grabbing a salad and a bowl of soup at the mall's food court.

Kayla made her final stop of the day the big pet supermarket where she could obtain the mosquito larvae that Angelfish Eve was so fond of. While in the store, she browsed through the displays of artificial driftwood and imitation rocks, searching for something that might be a suitable addition to Eve's tank.

As she reached for a package of the driftwood, her gaze landed on a miniature castle that was sandwiched between the displays. Kayla forgot about the driftwood. Picking up the castle, she inspected it. Like something out of a fairy tale, the castle was festooned with pastel pink and yellow trim, and it sported a tower with high windows and a large open door that an angelfish could easily swim through. On impulse, she decided to buy it.

Back at home, Kayla placed the castle in an empty spot near the front of the aquarium. She went to brew herself a cup of the hazelnut coffee and slice a piece from one of the cinnamon rolls. Then she stationed herself by the tank to watch Eve's reaction to the castle.

For a while Angelfish Eve swam in disinterested circles on the other side of the tank. Finally, curiosity won out, and the tiny fish approached the castle. She cautiously checked out the abode, front and back, then came to a standstill by the open door. Her dorsal fins fluttered, and she half-turned so that she appeared to be staring Kayla straight in the eye. Her mouth opened and closed, as if she were demanding, "So you bought me a castle. Now where is Prince Charming?"

"Well, Eve," Kayla said with a smile, "if I ever find him, I'll send him your way."

Prince Charming indeed. Kayla laughed at herself and popped the last bite of cinnamon roll into her mouth. Consulting her watch, she was relieved to see that it was almost three-thirty. Not too early to start getting ready for the party, she decided.

The nervousness she'd worked so hard to conquer during the course of the day returned with a vengeance the second she stepped into the shower. Even the steady stream of warm water against the muscles of her back failed to ease the knot of tension that was lodged between her shoulder blades.

Later, standing in front of the mirror in her bedroom, Kayla noticed that her hands were trembling as she applied her makeup. She had to redo her lipstick twice because her fumbling fingers missed their mark and the color went outside the line of her lips.

She stared briefly out the window in an effort to calm herself. The row of leafless, black trees that skirted the parking lot looked as vulnerable as her heart felt at that moment. She could no longer deny that the feelings Ryan's kiss had wakened in her put her former schoolgirl crush on him to shame. Wasn't that why she'd launched herself into a whirlwind of activity that day — to avoid having to own up to her burgeoning attraction to her partner?

How could one minute of bliss unleash such a Pandora's box of conflicting emotions? First she was dreaming of Ryan holding her close in the moonlight of a cold winter's night. In the next heartbeat, she was chastising herself for allowing her imagination to take such dangerous twists and turns. She didn't need a love affair with a man who had a reputation as a heartbreaker — or with any other man — to lead a happy and fulfilled life. A plum contract with a prestigious touring company would nicely take care of that.

With a sigh, she turned back to the

mirror and began to pile her dark hair into a loose twist, leaving a few tendrils free to trail around her ears and down the back of her neck. She secured the twist with a pearl-encrusted comb and examined the results in the mirror. Then she put on her new sweater and skirt and slipped her feet into her black leather dress boots.

After scrutinizing her reflection in the mirror a final time, she dabbed her favorite perfume — a sophisticated floral scent — behind her ears and on the pulse points of her neck and wrists. Then, closing her eyes, she massaged her temples in an attempt to conjure soothing images in her mind.

A sharp rap at the front door banished any soothing images. Her eyes flew open, and she checked the time. It was 5 p.m. on the dot. *Here goes,* she told herself.

Taking a deep breath, she opened the door. But when her gaze connected with Ryan's, the simple "hello" she meant to say got caught in her throat. If the slightly dazed expression on his face was any indication, it appeared he'd lost his powers of speech, too.

Well, Angelfish Eve, Kayla thought wildly, *I just found Prince Charming on my doorstep.* She gave herself a mental shake even as she took inventory of her partner's appearance.

Clad in black suede, from his jacket to his slacks, Ryan exuded princely charm from every pore. Underneath the jacket, a sapphire blue cable-knit sweater spanned his chest in an enticing way. His hair had been neatly trimmed. Still, the dark, wavy locks managed to skim the collar of his jacket in a reckless manner.

Veiled by thick lashes, Ryan's eyes commanded Kayla's attention until finally she tore her gaze from his. "Come in," she said at last. "I . . . only need to get my coat and I'm ready."

As soon as Ryan stepped inside, her nostrils picked up the musky, manly odor of his cologne. The scent was a marked contrast to the spicy after-shave he usually wore.

He cleared his throat. "This is for you," he said, bringing one hand out from behind his back. In his palm was an oblong box tied with a crimson ribbon.

"Another gift?"

"Just something for you to wear tonight."

Removing the lid, she discovered an orchid corsage. The white bloom was set against a background of delicate emerald green leaves. "It's beautiful. . . ."

He took the box from her hands and removed the corsage. She watched, slightly mesmerized, while he pinned the flower in just the right spot on her sweater. *No doubt he's had lots of practice,* she told herself. But she noticed that his fingers shook as he made a minor adjustment in the corsage, and he looked past her rather than at her when he was finished with the task.

Kayla cast about for something to say. Her gaze wandered to the aquarium. "If we have a minute, I want to show you what I bought Eve."

The corners of his mouth hinted at a smile. "We have more than a minute. Show me."

"This." She pointed to the castle where Eve was swimming in lazy circles around one of the turrets.

"Hmmm. Nice little house." Ryan hunkered down so that he was eye level with Eve and the castle. He drummed his fingers gently against the glass of the tank. "I'd say that Eve's happy with your choice."

Kayla crouched beside her partner, grateful for the diversion that Eve provided. "I wonder if I made a mistake in buying such a huge aquarium. Eve looks sort of lost, don't you think?"

"Yeah, now that you mention it. Maybe what she needs is some company to cheer her up."

"I was thinking that, too."

The silence grew deafening between them as they watched Eve dart in and out of the castle door. "We'd better go," Ryan said at last. Unexpectedly, he took hold of Kayla's hand and helped her to her feet.

"I'll get my coat," she said, trying to ignore the pleasurable tingle that radiated up her arm from where Ryan's fingers had curved around hers.

Kayla took advantage of the minute alone to compose herself. She drew in a couple of deep breaths, snatched up her coat, and returned to the living room.

"I'll take that," Ryan said, reaching for her coat.

She tried to smile, but her lips felt parched. She moistened them with her tongue. Glancing up, she caught Ryan's gaze focused on her mouth, and she moved ahead of him into the hallway. He took the key from her and locked the door to her apartment. But he didn't offer her his arm or so much as glance at her as they walked to the elevator. *It's going to be one long night if things don't loosen up soon.*

Ryan held the steering wheel steady and stared out the front window of the BMW into the gathering dusk. All the way up the winding road that led into the mountains west of the city, he and Kayla had ridden along without talking. Unless he wanted to count his trite comment about the state of the weather and her strained remark about how the developers were ruining the villages of Cascade and Green Mountain Falls.

Maneuvering the BMW around one of the hairpin turns that defined the mountain highway, he blamed himself for the tense manner in which their evening had begun. If only Kayla hadn't blown him away, looking so beautiful in that white sweater and red skirt that hugged every line of her elegant skater's body. If only he hadn't let his control slip again and allowed his eyes to feast on her loveliness like a starving man who'd been led to the banquet table. If only the smell of her perfume hadn't hit him full force, muddling his senses.

Enough of "if only's," he told himself. He'd started the evening with the best of intentions. He honestly wanted Kayla to have a good time at the party; he wanted to have a good time himself. Further, he wanted to make amends for any grief he'd caused her over these past few months because he'd acted more like a jerk than the conscientious partner she'd been accustomed to. His relationship with Christy was history, but he still regretted the worry he'd put Kayla through.

His hands clutched the steering wheel more tightly. Things had to be different now. It was time to get down to the serious business of claiming a couple of championships. Surely he could hang in there, keep a lid on his emotions for a little longer. Then Kayla would be well on her way to a pro career. And he would be . . .

"Ryan?"

Kayla's voice drew him out of his thoughts. He hadn't cared for the direction they were taking him anyway. "What?" With an action that was almost reflexive, he covered her hand with his. Her fingers were cold, and he didn't fight the urge to warm them.

"Didn't we just pass the turnoff to the lodge?"

Ryan jerked to attention and pulled his hand away from hers. A check in the rearview mirror proved she was right. As luck would have it, there was a café at the next bend in the road. Ryan swung his car into the parking lot and did a quick turnaround. Backtracking, he located the gravel lane with the sign beside it that read TIMBERFROST LODGE.

The lane as well as the fields on either side were coated with snow. For the first time since they'd left the Springs, Ryan noticed that there was a definite chill in the air. Even if it had felt more like fall today in the city, winter had taken up residence in the Rockies. And Kayla'd had the good sense to bring a coat along.

His partner always came prepared. The idea made him smile. But when he caught sight of the hotel looming at the end of the lane, its windows blazing with light, he felt suddenly unprepared to face the evening ahead, or to deal with the emotions that threatened to send all his finer instincts packing.

Chapter Eight

The view of Timberfrost Lodge set against the backdrop of the Rockies never failed to impress Kayla. But this evening, flecked with golden light beneath the dusky sky, the sight of the grand old hotel took on a larger-than-life quality in her eyes, as if it were the Colorado equivalent of some ancient storybook castle. Above the roof of the lodge, a full moon hung like a silver pendant in the heavens, while below the headlights of the cars moving slowly up the circular driveway resembled a bright strand of jewels in the deepening night.

As Ryan pulled in to join the line of cars, Kayla returned his tentative smile. They'd barely spoken to each other on the ride through the mountains, and Kayla was wise enough to know that it would take more than the romantic setting of Timberfrost Lodge to ease the tension between them. Did he regret asking her to accompany him, despite his thoughtful gesture of the corsage? She almost wished she had refused his invitation and come alone. Or on the arm of Hamil Brookings.

It's too late now, she told herself as Ryan brought the car to a halt.

A valet appeared at the passenger door of the BMW. "Good evening, Miss Quinn," he said with a polite nod, holding out a white-gloved hand to her.

She returned the valet's greeting. A chilly blast of wind hit her face when she emerged from the car, carrying with it a flurry of snowflakes. The valet hurried around to the other side of the BMW and opened the driver's side door for Ryan. The next thing Kayla knew, Ryan was beside her, helping her into her coat. His hand stayed at her elbow while they made their way to the veranda of the lodge, exchanging hellos and smiles with the other couples who were on their way toward the lobby.

"Watch your step," Ryan said once.

When she looked down, she saw that there was a slick spot in front of her on the veranda stairs. As she moved around the spot, she was conscious of the way Ryan's fingers tightened protectively around her arm.

Kayla recognized most of the people they met. Two — Marty Greenwell and Zack Randall — were judges. Others were coaches with their mates or select members of the press who had been extended a special invitation to the event.

Marty, tall, brunette, and fortyish, took Kayla's hand as they passed through the carved wooden doors of the lodge. "What a beautiful sweater, Kayla. And what an attractive corsage." Marty raised a finely shaped eyebrow and smiled at Ryan. Then she was gone, and Kayla lost sight of her in the crowd.

Kayla liked Marty, and she knew the woman held definite sympathies toward the team of Quinn and Maxwell. It was no secret that she loved the pair's program.

"There's one to keep track of," Ryan said.

"You mean Marty?"

He nodded. "We'll find her later."

"And Zack, too." Kayla nudged her partner's arm to draw his attention to the suave gray-haired man who stood a few feet away. *That's why we're here together,* she reminded herself, *to make small talk with the judges and smile sweetly for the press.*

The sponsors of the party formed a reception line in the lodge's palatially appointed lobby. Kayla received a succession of breathless hugs and polite kisses from the women as she moved through the line.

"How lovely you look, Kayla," gushed white-haired Edith Blumberg, a very wealthy — and influential — fan of the local skating community.

"So wonderful to see you," breathed a heavily perfumed Marion Hutchinson, as she drew Kayla into her ample arms.

Glancing at her partner, Kayla noticed that even he hadn't escaped the ladies' clutches. There was a bright crimson stain on his cheek, evidence of Edith's smooch. "Wait, Ryan," she said. She pulled a tissue from her purse and wiped the smudge from his face.

Ryan caught her hand in his and snatched up the tissue. He took a step closer to her as if there were a lot more on his mind than disposing of a soiled Kleenex. "Let's see if your corsage survived the crushing blows."

His fingers lightly grazed the flower, and Kayla imagined them stroking her cheek instead. She watched as he broke off a damaged tendril and tossed it along with the tissue into a nearby wastebasket.

"There," he whispered. Their eyes met,

and neither of them moved for a couple of breaths.

Help, thought Kayla. How were they ever going to make it through dinner — let alone an evening of lighthearted chitchat with an assemblage of shrewd-eyed judges?

As if he'd read her mind, Ryan glanced away. "We'd better go in," he said.

They left Kayla's coat at the check-in counter and moved on to the hotel's cavernous dining room.

"It looks like the chef outdid himself this year," Ryan observed.

Buffet tables adorned with elaborate ice sculptures and vases of fresh flowers lined two walls of the room. But somehow the tables laden with sumptuous dishes failed to stimulate Kayla's appetite. She peered up to find Ryan staring at her instead of the food. "Do you want to eat now?" she asked.

"If you do," he said.

Soft laughter and the hum of conversation swirled around her. From a distance she heard the strains of an orchestra tuning up; the sound reminded her that later there would be dancing in the adjacent ballroom. In years past Ryan had traditionally asked her for the last dance of the evening, and it had been a running joke between them that they both seemed to sprout two left feet whenever they attempted to dance together.

Suddenly the idea of tripping over Ryan's feet as he held her in his arms struck Kayla as far more romantic than funny. But how did *he* feel about it? His expression was guarded, and she feared he was contemplating dispensing with tradition and keeping a careful distance from her.

A familiar voice intruded on Kayla's thoughts, and she turned to find Mitchell Porter waving at her. The tall, well-built men's singles skater called out a greeting.

"Come join us," he said. He was balancing a plate of food in one hand. With the other, he motioned toward Justin, who was heading for a linen-clothed guest table.

"Who'd you see?" Ryan asked beside her.

"Mitchell." She began to fill a plate with green salad from a cut-glass bowl. "He wants us to join him and Justin."

"Fine," he said without enthusiasm.

Kayla scanned the crowd for any sign of a mop of curly red hair. "I wonder where Meghan and Scott are."

"They aren't coming until later."

"What?" Kayla stopped, her fork poised over a large, chilled shrimp. "How do you know that?"

Ryan heaped his plate with salad. "Because I had breakfast with Scott this morning, and he told me he was taking Meghan to Sunstone for dinner."

"Why Sunstone?"

Ryan shrugged. "I guess you'll have to ask them when they get here."

Kayla jabbed her fork into the shrimp. Why should she feel irked because Ryan hadn't told her the news before? It hardly mattered. Nearly any topic that came up between them these days seemed to set off a sensitive nerve in one or the other of them. The closed expression on Ryan's face told her that it would be an exercise in futility to press him further on the subject of Meghan and Scott's dining habits that particular evening.

Surveying the crowd again, Kayla's throat tightened when she caught sight of a woman's blond head across the room. Sooner or later, she and Ryan were bound to run into Christy. She just hoped it was later. But then the woman turned, and Kayla saw that she'd been mistaken. The woman was older than Christy, a bit heavier, too. Still, Kayla couldn't help but wonder how Ryan would react when he finally came face-to-face with his ex-girlfriend.

"Kayla?" Ryan regarded her quizzically.

"What?"

He frowned slightly. "Nothing."

They made their way in silence to Mitchell and Justin's table. Without asking, Ryan took her plate and set it next to his, then pulled out her chair for her.

"Wow!" Justin gave a low whistle in Kayla's direction.

Mitchell leaned his elbows on the table. "Hey Maxwell, you're a lucky guy, you know."

Ryan's demeanor didn't exactly give the impression that he thought he was a "lucky guy," Kayla noticed. He appeared to ignore the remark as he bent his head over his plate and lifted a forkful of salad to his mouth.

"I'm starved," Kayla said, though nothing could have been further from the truth.

"Me, too," Ryan muttered, not looking up.

"The buffet's terrific," Justin put in.

"So is the view," Mitchell quipped, winking at Kayla.

She forced a smile, telling herself to

lighten up. The two men were only engaged in a little game of harmless flirting with her.

"Look who's making his grand entrance, Kayla." Mitchell gave her arm a tap.

She glanced up in time to see Fletcher strike a dramatic pose in the doorway of the dining room. His fire-engine red sportscoat was a show-stopper, and he had the usual gaggle of adoring young skaters hanging on his coattails. The kids, most just into their teens, idolized the deposed men's champion. Consensus among the seasoned skaters was that the kids were hoping that some of Fletcher's flair for the theatrical would rub off on them. Ryan had nicknamed the assemblage the "Kiddie Club."

"Someone ought to tell them that hanging around ol' Fletch is bad news."

"Ryan and I have tried, Jus'," Mitchell countered. "But what can I say? They're in awe of Godwin." He raised his arms in a gesture of mock homage to Fletcher.

"You know," Ryan said, "at least one person is benefiting from that adulation."

They all laughed, but Kayla's sense of humor fled when she felt Ryan's thigh brush against hers under the table. She was sure the contact was accidental, but its effect on her was far from innocent. Peering over at Ryan, she observed a man who seemed to be relishing his meal, unaware of the pleasurable tremors his touch provoked in her.

The topic of conversation switched from Fletcher to judges and their methods of sizing up a competition. Kayla finally joined in, but her thoughts were scattered, and her tongue refused to cooperate. The one comment she made came out embarrassingly garbled. She'd wanted to say "fair," but it had come out "pair" — to the amusement of her three companions.

With a sense of relief, she heard Ryan say, "Are you finished with your dinner or do you want to go for seconds?"

"No seconds. I'm full."

"You didn't eat much," Ryan pointed to the seafood in pastry that had smelled so tempting on the buffet table.

"I wasn't as hungry as I thought," she retorted.

"Let's go then."

"Leaving us so soon?" Mitchell asked.

"We're going to bend the ears of a few judges."

Kayla would never have imagined she'd be so anxious to seek out the judges.

"Good idea, Ryan," Justin agreed. "I

think I'll find Chelsea and do the same."

"You mean you're deserting me, too, Jus'?" Mitchell said with a fake wounded look. He turned to Kayla. "Save a dance for me, will you?"

"Sorry, but her dance card is filled for the evening."

Ryan's clipped reply took Kayla by such surprise that she had no chance to respond.

Mitchell laughed. "Hey, I didn't realize . . ." He smoothed his hair back. "Well, you two have fun." He picked up his knife and fork and began to tackle the piece of chicken that was on his plate.

Ryan was already steering her away from the table when Kayla dug in her heel and stopped. "Mitchell," she called. He raised his eyes. "I'll save a dance for you," she said with a sharp look in Ryan's direction.

When they were out of earshot of the table, Ryan pulled her aside. "Don't you know that Mitch has a crush on you?"

"A crush? What makes you think that?"

"I'd say it's pretty plain to see."

"Not to me." She'd never remotely considered the idea. Where had Ryan come up with the notion? "But what right," she asked, "did you have to say that my dance card was filled?"

His jaw clenched in a stubborn line. "No right, I suppose."

He strode on, and Kayla had to run to catch up. "What about you?" she challenged. "Don't tell me you're going to break with your time-honored tradition of dancing with every woman on the premises."

"I'd planned on that, yes." Suddenly he turned and grasped her by the shoulders. His eyes pinned hers. "Do you mind so much if I'm your only partner, Kayla?"

Gazing into those dark, earnest eyes, she had to bite back the confession that she'd never wanted anyone else to be her partner. *And I never will.*

"Ah, if it isn't our very own Sir Galahad."

Kayla gasped. She twisted away from Ryan and found Fletcher's pale eyes coldly assessing her.

"And here we have the fair princess," Fletcher said.

The "Kiddie Club" closed ranks around their hero and collectively gaped at Kayla and Ryan. Kayla searched for some clever reply that would bring Fletcher down a peg or two. Glimpsing her partner, she saw a sly smile spread across his face.

"And here, Kayla," he said with a bow in

Fletcher's direction, "we have the royal toad."

Fletcher's eyes widened and his mouth fell open. Several members of the "Kiddie Club" began to giggle.

Kayla dissolved in laughter as Ryan escorted her around the speechless former champion. "I think that's the first time I've seen Fletcher at a loss for words," she said.

Her partner grinned. "If I have any say about the matter, it won't be the last."

Kayla had to admire the smooth way Ryan had handled the incident. And the interlude had served to cool some of the heat building between them. Poor Fletcher would never know that he'd done them a favor by his obnoxious presence.

"There's Marty and Zack."

Kayla followed Ryan's gaze and spotted the two judges who were seated at a table by themselves. "Do you think this is a good time to pay them a visit?"

"As good a time as any," Ryan said, letting her go ahead of him.

Zack rose at their approach. "Ryan." He held out his hand and gave Ryan's a healthy shake. "Kayla." He directed a gracious nod her way. "Why don't you sit down?"

They sat, Ryan beside Zack, Kayla next to Marty.

"So how's it going with you two?" Zack tossed the question to Ryan.

Ryan seemed to hesitate before picking up the conversational ball. "We're having to iron out a few kinks in our program. But it's coming along, wouldn't you say, Kayla?"

She paused a second too long. "Yes, I'd say we're making progress." While the statement might not be a blatant lie, she wished she had the confidence to tell the judges that everything was dandy with the team of Quinn and Maxwell.

Silence fell around the table. Kayla folded her hands in front of her. Ryan gave a short cough. Zack lifted his water glass to his mouth. And Marty smiled.

"I loved the costumes you wore the other day," Marty said.

Was our performance so abysmal that Marty is reduced to grabbing at straws? Kayla wondered.

"And you skated extraordinarily well." Marty's comment sounded suspiciously like an afterthought.

"Yes, a marvelous program," Zack enthused.

Bless you, Zack. "Thank you. We have a lot of hard work ahead of us yet."

"A whole heck of a lot," Ryan concurred.

Marty ran a perfectly manicured finger-nail around the rim of her glass. "I heard about Eve's brother-in-law," she said with a frown. "I'm sorry."

"It was a pretty bad shock," Ryan admitted. "We saw her off at the airport yesterday."

"A darn shame," Zack lamented. "But family crises never seem to respect a schedule."

No, thought Kayla, *and this one was especially ill-timed.* Still, she couldn't fault Eve. The coach had to help out her sister.

"We'll be adding extra practices in the meantime," Ryan said.

Marty nodded. "I'd like to make a suggestion."

"What's that?" Kayla asked, suddenly alert.

Marty smiled. Counsel was always easier to take when it was dished out artfully. "I think your program would be even more impressive if you changed your second triple loop to a triple Lutz and added another triple Salchow."

Ryan's expression was neutral as he turned to Zack. "What's your opinion, Zack?"

"I have to agree with Marty."

"Kayla?" Ryan leaned his elbows on the

table and met her eyes.

She didn't know what to say. It was common for skaters to make changes in their routines up to — and including — the day of the competition itself. But, given the problems they'd been having lately, she wondered if it wasn't a risky proposition to begin toying with their long program. "It's something to consider," she acknowledged.

Ryan pushed his chair back. "We'll give it serious thought, Marty." He and Zack shook hands again.

"You really do look wonderful tonight, Kayla." Marty glanced in Ryan's direction. "Both of you."

"So do you." Kayla meant it; Marty was a very attractive woman.

Ryan came around the table and clasped Marty's outstretched hand. She held his hand for a moment between hers. "Have fun," she said. Then she turned to Zack and the two of them strolled away, arm-in-arm.

Kayla looked at her partner. "Do you suppose that they're . . . an item?"

His arm took possession of her waist. "Appears that way to me," he said.

What do we do now? she thought. The strains of a familiar pop ballad floated through the air, and Kayla realized they had drifted near the entrance to the ballroom. Ryan didn't ask if she wanted to go in, and she hated to make the suggestion. But the truth was that she'd much rather be dancing with him at the moment than rubbing elbows with more judges.

She shook herself. The conversation with Marty and Zack should have served as a wake-up call to her. If she allowed herself to be seduced by her partner's charms, wouldn't she regret it in the cold light of morning when they found themselves back on the ice at the arena?

But, she argued with herself, what harm was there in having a little fun as long as she remembered to keep her feelings in check? Yet how could she trust herself to stay emotionally distanced from her partner when the merest brush of his fingers on her skin sent quivers through her?

She guessed that Ryan was carrying on his own inner debate, wrestling with the idea of going on into the ballroom as opposed to searching out the other judges. Finally, duty won out, and they spent the next hour circling the dining room and lobby.

While none of the remaining judges made any pointed recommendations about their program, one did remind Kayla and Ryan that "unison is everything in pairs skating." Another told them with a contrived smile that he would be watching for "passion and precision" in their long program.

The judge with the condescending air was Kayla's least favorite among the officials. She'd always doubted his ability to judge fairly. Yet all she could do was act gracious toward him and bide her time until he chose to take his leave.

After what seemed an eternity, the judge turned away. Blowing a kiss at Kayla, he wished the two of them "all good success." She heard Ryan heave a sigh.

"I think we've earned some down time," he said, burying his face in her hair. "How about a dance?"

The intimacy of his request, his mouth pressed against her hair, caused all rational thought to flee. Forgetting her resolve to keep her emotions in check, she brought her fingers up to stroke his chin. "I'd like that," she whispered.

Ryan started to say something, then suddenly he raised his head. "They're here," he said in a husky voice.

"Who . . ." Kayla looked across the room and saw Meghan and Scott. The couple, all smiles, was headed in their direction.

Chapter Nine

From the looks of it, things had gone very well, Ryan surmised as he watched Scott and Meghan. Scott was beaming from ear to ear, and when Meghan reached up to plant a kiss on his cheek, he nearly lifted the bride-to-be off her feet. Next thing, he'd be carrying her across the room.

"They look happy, don't they, Ryan?"

"Yeah, they do." *Kayla sounds kind of wistful,* he thought. Maybe he should've told her about the proposal. No, he'd made a promise to Scott. Besides, Meghan was the right person to break the news to Kayla since they were best friends.

"Hey, bud." Scott offered a crooked grin.

Ryan took his buddy's hand in a firm clasp. From the corner of his eye, he saw Kayla embracing Meghan.

"We're going to the ladies' lounge," Meghan announced.

"Okay." Scott placed a fast kiss on her lips.

"I'll be back in a couple of minutes, Ryan."

"Sure, Kayla." He stood watching her, entertaining the notion that in a few minutes he would be holding her close on the dance floor.

"I see you bought Kayla a corsage."

"What?" Ryan faced his friend. "Oh, the orchid. I figured she might like it."

"Did she?"

"Seemed to. But hey . . . I'm not the one getting hitched. How'd it go?"

"I barely got the question out before Meggy said yes."

"She'll make you a great wife, Scott." For some strange reason, he had a hard time getting the words out.

"Are you and Kayla enjoying yourselves?"

Ryan hesitated. How could she be enjoying herself when he'd been acting like a possessive jerk who'd practically ordered her not to dance with anyone but him? "We just got done doing our duty with the judges. Now we're ready for a couple of dances." *At least* I'm *ready,* he should have said. *More than ready.*

"I have to tell you, bud, I think Kayla

likes your company a heck of a lot more than you realize. Or than you're willing to own up to."

Ryan evaded his friend's steady gaze. "How come you keep wanting to talk about Kayla and me when you're the lucky guy who got engaged?"

Scott gave a chuckle. "No particular reason."

Ryan seized the opportunity to shift the topic of conversation away from himself and Kayla and onto the safe subject of food.

"Here they come," Scott interrupted, as if he hadn't been listening to Ryan's litany about the variety of eats available on the buffet tables.

All thoughts of food fled Ryan's head too when he saw Kayla making her way back to him. His eyes were drawn to her like a man is drawn to a fire on a cold winter's night, and he waged an unsuccessful battle against the urge to fasten his arm around her waist the instant she took her place at his side. At least he had the presence of mind to offer a word of congratulations to Meghan.

"Thanks, Ryan."

Meghan's freckle-dusted face wore an attractive glow of happiness, he noticed. But his attention didn't stray long from his partner. "Are you ready for that dance now?" he said.

Why was her pretty mouth curving down instead of up? Was she perturbed at him because he hadn't clued her in on the good news about Meghan and Scott?

"You know I was sworn to secrecy about the engagement," he said.

"Meghan told me," she said, without making eye contact. She extended her hand to Scott. "I'm really happy for both of you."

She didn't sound all that happy, Ryan considered. But if she was still upset with him, he'd draw a smile from her once they were on the dance floor. "You two coming?" he asked Scott.

"Not just yet. We didn't have dessert at Sunstone, so we're going to check out the buffet."

Ryan put on a grin for his friend as he guided Kayla toward the ballroom. From the loudness of the music, it appeared the orchestra was in full swing. But he sensed that Kayla was holding back for some reason.

"What's wrong?" he said. Was she about to refuse to dance with him? Tracking her gaze, he saw at once what the problem was.

Christy stood only a few yards away, hanging on Vancoff's arm. But worse than that, she was staring straight at Ryan.

"Christy's with Sully," his partner whispered as if he hadn't recognized the flashy agent.

"That's okay with me."

It didn't seem so okay when Christy started making a beeline for them, with Vancoff in tow.

"Ryan, how nice to see you," Christy said with the most insincere smile he'd ever seen. She was dressed in a slinky blue off-the-shoulder number that left little to the imagination. Her gaze cruised over him from head to toe as if he were stripped down to nothing but his boxer shorts.

"Hi," he said, hoping that would be the end of the conversation. It was only after Kayla gave him a quick jab in the ribs that he realized Vancoff had offered him his hand. "How's it going, Sully?" he asked, managing to sound civil.

"Terrific, as always. How about you, Maxwell?"

"Just great." Ryan noted that Vancoff's blond hair was about as long as Christy's. Didn't the guy believe in haircuts? Ryan had to admit he was prejudiced. He'd never much liked the agent, had figured him to be in a class with Brookings. He decided now that his opinion hadn't changed. But he did conclude that Vancoff and Christy were a perfect match for each other.

"And Kayla. You look *so* lovely."

Christy's compliment sounded as phony as the diamond choker she wore around her neck.

"You too, Christy."

They all eyed each other. The air was so thick that Ryan was sure he could have diced it into pieces with the blades of his skates if he'd had them handy.

Christy gave a delicate cough. "I just love your outfit, Kayla. It's absolutely adorable. Did you knit the sweater yourself? Or is it another one of your finds?" She glanced at Sully and toyed with a strand of her hair. "Kayla gets the biggest thrill out of haunting the bargain basement at Bingman's. You just never know what quaint little number she'll show up in next."

Ryan felt Kayla stiffen at his side. A rush of protective anger consumed him. "Cut it, Christy." His eyes sent her a stony warning.

"Why, Ryan, what did I say?" She shrugged those elegant shoulders of hers.

"Oh, Sully, some people can't take a perfectly innocent joke." Sighing, she looped her arm through the agent's and marched away.

There she goes again, thought Ryan, *leading another man around by the nose.* But his concern was only for Kayla. He took gentle hold of her arm. "You okay?" he asked.

"Fine. Just determined not to stoop to her level, that's all."

Ryan wasn't about to tell her this time that Christy meant no harm by her comment. He more than suspected that Christy was jealous of Kayla's wholesome beauty — and probably had been for a good long while. "Don't let her get under your skin," he whispered in Kayla's ear.

The orchestra started a new tune, and Ryan found an empty spot on the crowded dance floor. But before he and Kayla had a chance to take a step, they were accosted by a photographer from the local paper who wanted a picture. They consented, conscious that a photo in the newspaper was free publicity for them. The members of the media who were lucky enough to be invited to the party were expected to keep a low profile, allowing the guests some space to enjoy themselves without the fear of being cornered by a nosy reporter. But on occasion, a photographer or reporter slipped in who failed to honor the tradition.

The photographer was gracious enough. He took a few candid shots, thanked them for their time, and told them to look for a picture of themselves in the Sunday edition of *The Gazette-Telegraph.*

The orchestra was already into their next number, a smooth ballad. Ryan took Kayla's hand in his, put his other hand at her waist, and they began to move in time to the music. There was a moment or two when they narrowly missed tramping on each other's toes, but they were soon gliding around the floor as if dancing together was something they did every day. If Ryan didn't know better, he would have sworn they had skates on their feet instead of shoes.

Except this was different than skating. On the ice they were apart almost as much as they were together. Here, on the dance floor, their eyes caught and held; their hands and bodies were in constant contact.

An alarm went off in Ryan's mind, warning him to set a prudent distance between himself and Kayla. He tuned it out. Didn't he want to show her a good time?

But his reasoning rang hollow, even to himself. His body's response to her nearness told the true tale. He was the one having a good time.

When the melody ended, he gave no thought to releasing her. And Kayla didn't move away from him, only leaned back to look into his eyes. "The orchestra's better than the one last year, don't you think?"

"Much better than last year's," he agreed. His gaze focused on her mouth. He remembered the tantalizing taste of her lips, and a fire ignited deep inside his body.

Just in time, the orchestra struck up another tune, one with an up-tempo beat. Ryan let out a breath he hadn't realized he'd been holding as he started to lead Kayla through the steps of a dance that was the latest craze.

She put up her hands and laughed. "Sorry. I don't have a clue how to do this."

"It's easy. Just watch." Pivoting on his heel, he showed her the proper steps and turns. By the time he was finished, she was giggling. "Am I that bad?" he asked with a grin.

"No." Her eyes sparkled with humor. "You're wonderful," she said.

"Then why don't we see how wonderful

we can be together," he whispered against her hair.

After that, the orchestra launched into a string of nostalgic slow tunes. Twice, Ryan caught a glimpse of Mitchell headed their way — and twice he steered Kayla in the opposite direction. He knew Mitch's intent, and he wasn't about to step aside and watch Kayla dance with the tall singles skater. Or any other bachelor in the place, he concluded. He wanted to keep his partner all to himself that night.

They didn't talk much as they danced, but it seemed to Ryan that their eyes carried on a deeper dialogue, one that stoked the fire inside of him.

Once, during "The Unchained Melody," Kayla looked up and said, "Meghan asked me to be her maid of honor."

Ryan drew her hand to his chest and smiled. "I know. Scott asked me to be his best man."

"It kind of caught me off-guard," she said softly. Her hand hovered in the vicinity of his heart. "Their engagement, I mean. I know I shouldn't be surprised. They're obviously in love. But it just seems that . . . everything is happening so fast."

"I don't imagine they see it as too fast."

"I suppose not."

There was a little catch in her throat, and Ryan thought he saw the gleam of a tear in her eye. *Nah, it's my imagination,* he told himself, though he felt kind of sentimental too. What was wrong with them — getting all misty-eyed because their best friends were about to tie the knot?

But a force far more potent than sentimentality was at work on his emotions. Wisdom dictated that he and Kayla needed a time-out. Instead, he held her more tightly.

In the end, Ryan would have been hard-pressed to say what caused the last of his resolve to crumble into a pile of broken promises. It could have been the fragrance of Kayla's hair, like roses and rainwater, or the soft feel of the silky strands against his face. Or it might've been the way her hands came up to cradle his neck as they danced. Or maybe it was the trusting expression in her eyes when he paused to stroke back a strand of her hair that had come loose from the comb.

Whatever it was, Ryan managed to maneuver the two of them into a private spot amid a bunch of potted plants. The orchestra struck up the Mariah Carey song, "Forever," and Ryan knew that he was going to kiss Kayla. The temptation was overpowering to know the feel of her lips on his again. Her eyes, bright with longing as they gazed into his, told him that was what she wanted, too. He said her name, brought one hand up to rest against the satiny thickness of her hair. Paradise was his for the taking. As if in a dream, he cupped her chin in his other hand and began to lower his mouth to hers.

A flash of red crossed his line of vision like the warning signal at a railroad crossing, and he jerked back.

"What is it?" Confusion clouded the brightness in Kayla's eyes.

Ryan pulled her with him until they were concealed by a large fake fern. He drew a shaky breath. "Fletcher," he said. "And a reporter from the local paper," he added, spotting the news hound tagging after Fletcher.

Suddenly, Ryan wanted out of there. Away from Fletcher and the nosy press. Away from the dim lights and the romantic music that made him take leave of his senses. Away from the emotions that had tripped him up again and brought him to the brink of doing what he'd vowed not to do.

"Maxwell! How ya doing?" a commanding voice called out.

Ryan spun around so fast he almost lost his balance. Kayla gasped and leaned into him as he strained to see who had yelled to him. Whoever it was had gone on, but the surprise greeting moved him to action.

"Let's go," he said.

"You want to leave?"

Ignoring the wounded tone of Kayla's voice, he hoped she would follow his lead and not ask any more questions. Because he didn't have any answers. All he knew was that he was taking her home.

He didn't look at her or say a word until after he had retrieved her coat. She regarded him in sullen silence when he told her to wait for him while he went on a search for the valet. After the hunt proved futile, he decided to go for the car himself, and he ordered Kayla to stay put on the veranda until he brought the car around.

"No, I'm coming with you," she said with a stubborn tilt of her chin that brought her face close to his. Her breath heated his cheeks, his mouth in the bitterly cold air.

Don't, he silently warned her, fighting back the urge to kiss her long and hard right then and there. But she paid him no heed as she turned and started down the stairs.

Suddenly he recalled the slick spot on the step. She was headed right for it. He reached for her arm at the same time that he shouted for her to stop.

But it was too late. He saw her left heel come down, her foot begin to slide out from under. He made a desperate lunge for her, but his reflexes weren't fast enough, and before he could make another move, she crumpled onto the sidewalk in a little heap, clutching at her left leg.

"Kayla!" He knelt beside her, adrenaline pumping wildly through his veins as he smoothed loose tendrils of hair away from her face.

She gave a soft moan. "My ankle . . . I think I hurt it."

"Put your arms around my neck," Ryan ordered, and she obeyed. He lifted her off the sidewalk and carried her back up the steps and into the lobby. She felt as weightless as a bird in his arms as he gently laid her on the nearest sofa. Quickly he worked to remove the boot from her left foot. The ankle was already beginning to swell.

"It might be sprained." *Or broken,* he thought with a wave of panic. *Please let her be okay,* he prayed.

"Ryan!"

He jumped up at the sound of Meghan's voice. She was sprinting across the lobby in his direction.

"What on earth . . ." Meghan dropped down beside the sofa.

"I fell on the veranda steps," Kayla moaned, "and . . . hurt my ankle."

"Meghan . . ." Ryan touched her arm. "Where's Scott?"

Her eyes were big and shiny, as if she were about to cry. "I'll get him. Should I call for an ambulance?"

Kayla clasped Meghan's arm. "No! No ambulance."

Ryan shook his head. "I'll take her back to the Springs," he told Meghan. "What I need for you to do is bring me some crushed ice and a large towel. In a jiffy," he added.

"Right away," she agreed. "And I'll send Scotty to help too."

Ryan turned to his partner. "First, we have to see what kind of injury you have." He removed her other boot. "Can you stand?" he asked. She nodded, biting her lip. "I'll hold onto you."

She raised her chin. "I can get up by my-self."

Good, he thought with a small smile. *She can still sass me.* But she didn't argue with him when he draped her arm over his shoulder and told her that, on the count of three, they would rise together. "Don't put any weight on your left foot until I say," he cautioned her. He shifted his weight so that he had a more firm hold on her. "Try turning your ankle — slowly."

She did, twisting it to the left, then the right. "That's fine," he encouraged her. "Now put a little weight on it and see if you can take a few steps."

When she'd managed that, he asked, "Any numbness or tingling in your leg or foot?"

"No."

"Okay. I don't think you've broken any bones." He scooped her up in his arms and laid her back on the sofa.

"Ryan . . ."

Her fingers brushed his cheek; he captured them and pressed them to his mouth. "You're going to be all right," he said, praying that it was true.

"I'm so sorry. I was careless . . . mad at you," she said. She cast her eyes down. "I didn't watch where I was going."

"No, don't, Kayla." He wiped a tear from her cheek. She was tearing him up inside. He was dangerously close to losing control himself. "We've got to work fast, partner, get you back to the Springs." *Keep your cool, Maxwell.*

Scott came along just in time. "Meggy told me what happened," he said, crouching beside the sofa.

"I think the ankle's sprained," Ryan told his buddy. "See if you can dig up a first aid kit, would you? We could use an elastic bandage."

"I'm on my way."

Ryan proceeded to take off his shoes, then his socks.

"What are you doing?"

"Got to apply compression to the ankle to cut down on the swelling. So I'm making a sling for it."

"Out of your socks?"

She sounded so incredulous that he was able to smile. "Sure am. Just watch." He knotted the wool socks together and fashioned them into a horseshoe shape. "It's a trick Bill taught me. We'll fit this around the knob of the ankle." He showed her. "Then we'll wrap it all snug and secure in the bandage — or whatever Scott manages to scavenge for us." He darted a glance behind him. *Hurry, Scott. Time's wasting.*

As if he had telepathy, Scott appeared,

holding the bandage aloft. But his mouth gaped open when he saw Ryan's bare feet. "What in the . . ."

"He made a sling out of his socks," Kayla explained.

Scott chuckled. "Well, here's the Ace." He dropped the rolled-up bandage into Ryan's hands.

"Thanks, buddy." Ryan positioned the folded socks around the knob. "Hold this in place, will you, Scott?" When Scott had a grip on the makeshift sling, Ryan wrapped the entire ankle in the elastic. After a couple of adjustments, he leaned back on his heels. "There, that ought to keep it secure until we get to the hospital."

"Hospital?"

"I'm taking you to Penrose. We've got to . . ."

"No! You said yourself that nothing's broken." As soon as she'd spoken, Kayla must have realized how foolish her protest was. "Okay," she said with a sigh.

Ryan was relieved at her compliance. How could he have had any peace of mind, wondering if he'd been wrong about the extent of the injury? But could he have peace of mind anyway, after what had happened that evening? "Scott. Would you mind bringing my car around?"

No sooner had Scott left than Meghan returned. "I've got a huge towel and crushed ice in a plastic bag — courtesy of the kitchen."

"Great, Meghan. If you could hold onto them for a few minutes until Scott gets here with my car."

Meghan embraced Kayla. "You'll be all right. You're in very good hands." Her eyes met Ryan's.

Meghan could have no idea how much her words condemned him. But he kept his voice calm when he told Kayla, "We'll pack the ankle in the ice just as soon as we get you in the car." Then, before she could reply, he got up and went to wait for Scott, half sick with worry and placing the blame squarely on himself for the disastrous turn their evening had taken.

Chapter Ten

"You're a fortunate young woman." Dr. Abel Quintana, the emergency room physician, regarded Kayla over his glasses. Behind him were four backlit X rays of her ankle and foot. "Your X rays show no broken bones or hairline fractures. You've suffered a minor lateral sprain. What that means is you fell with your foot turned in, pulling ligaments on the outside of your ankle."

Kayla was tempted to tell Ryan that he'd been right. There were no broken bones. She glanced sideways at him from where she sat in a chair with her ankle propped up. His brow was furrowed, his mouth drawn into a thin line. She knew he'd been shaken up by her fall, and he still looked worried, despite the doctor's assurances. She decided to save the "I told you so's" for later.

Besides, she suspected there were other

matters weighing on his mind — like the memory of that moment when he seemed about to kiss her behind the potted plants and she had been like a piece of clay in his hands, ready for molding.

Ryan gave a slight cough. "That's good news then, isn't it?" he said.

Dr. Quintana smiled. "Yes, and you deserve a lot of the credit, Ryan." He directed his attention to Kayla. "Your partner did exactly the right thing. Wrapping the ankle and applying ice to the injury has already served to minimize swelling. The fact you're in superb athletic condition is a plus, too. I foresee you starting some therapy tomorrow."

"Does that mean I can practice in the afternoon?"

Dr. Quintana held up his hand and laughed. "Not so fast, Kayla. I didn't mean strenuous exercise. I want you to use alternate warm and cold baths on the ankle the first thing each morning for the next few days. Four minutes in the warm — not hot — water to one minute in the cold."

"Anything else we should do?"

Kayla didn't miss the "we" in Ryan's question.

"Yes," the doctor continued. "Kayla, while your foot and ankle are submersed in the warm bath, move your ankle around — side to side, up and down. Pretend you're writing the alphabet with your big toe."

She caught Ryan smiling, and her spirits were lifted a little, despite the pain shooting through her leg. "I'm not planning on missing the Golden Skates for a sprained ankle," she warned.

"I can see that you've got a great deal of determination," the physician said. "There's no reason for you to miss the competition — if you take good care of the ankle for several days. You wouldn't be the first skater — the first athlete, for that matter — to compete with an ankle injury." He pushed his glasses up on his nose. "I remember when John Alexander won the men's competition at the arena skating on a sprained ankle. I should know, because I was an intern at the time and helped treat the injury. That was in '72."

The name of the skater sounded vaguely familiar to Kayla. She wondered if Eve had been acquainted with John during her amateur days.

"Then there was Margie Wilhelms," Dr. Quintana continued. "She twisted her ankle a week and a half before the Golden Skates in '78. She skated her heart out and won the women's title handily. The point is that your injury shouldn't bar you from competing. *If* you follow my advice," he emphasized. Turning to Ryan, he said, "Will you make sure that Kayla stays off the ice until Tuesday?"

"Tuesday," Kayla groaned.

Ryan looked her in the eye. "I'll make sure," he promised.

She knew better than to carry her complaint any further. And there were things she couldn't say in the presence of the doctor. How could she and Ryan afford to miss even a single practice when their short and long programs needed their urgent attention? How could she assuage the guilt that squeezed at her heart and made her chest feel as if it were crushed?

"I'm going to give you a prescription for a painkiller and mild relaxant," Dr. Quintana said. He strode over to a small desk. "If you have a stationary bicycle, Kayla, you can start pedaling a mile or so on it tomorrow."

"I don't have a bicycle. Could I walk instead?"

"Walking would be fine, too."

"You can borrow my bike," Ryan offered. His gaze held hers. "I'll bring it over to your apartment first thing in the morning."

After the doctor had finished writing the prescription and had cautioned her to keep the ankle wrapped when she resumed practice, Ryan helped Kayla out to his car and bundled her into the front seat. Then he ran back in to get the prescription filled at the hospital's all-night pharmacy.

Conveniently, Kayla lived just a few blocks from the hospital, and it was only a matter of minutes before Ryan brought the BMW to a smooth stop in front of the brick apartment building.

"Don't try to get out," he ordered her. In a jiffy, he was on her side of the car, lifting her in his arms.

She clamped her mouth shut and secured her arms around his neck. Letting him take charge for the moment, she closed her eyes and pressed her cheek against his jacket as he carried her into the lobby and over to the elevator.

Despite a couple of murmured protests on her part, Ryan refused to put her down until they reached her apartment. Once inside, he gently deposited her on the sofa.

"Thank you . . . for everything," she said. Ryan's face was hidden from her as he plumped up the cushions behind her back and shoulders. *He's got to be exhausted, too,* she thought. Checking her watch, she saw it was 1:30 a.m. "You'd better go home. It's already Saturday morning."

Ryan knelt beside the sofa. "You think I'm going home?" He shook his head. "No way. I'm staying right here."

Here? In her apartment? That was ridiculous. "But . . . you can't," she said.

"Why not? After I've made you a snack and seen that you've taken one of your pills, then you can go to bed, and I'll be nearby in case you need anything."

I'll be nearby. . . . The memory of his kiss in the parking lot outside Estelle's, the image of his face so close to hers in the ballroom at Timberfrost Lodge, blazed in her mind. "I can't let you do that," she argued. "You need your sleep, Ryan."

"Well, this sofa should be a pretty comfortable place to bunk," he countered. He regarded her with a crooked smile. "Your corsage looks about as tired as you do."

Until he mentioned it, Kayla had forgotten about the corsage. She gazed with dismay at the flower. The orchid was half crushed, the shiny leaves bent and torn.

"I'll toss it out," Ryan offered. He started to undo the pin on the corsage.

"No, don't throw it away."

His eyebrows arched in surprise. "Why

not? The flower's a goner, I'm afraid."

Would he think she was crazy if she told him that she wanted to keep it — for reasons she didn't quite understand herself? "Just put it in the refrigerator. Please, Ryan."

He shrugged. "Whatever you want."

While he toted the orchid off to the refrigerator, Kayla thought once more of that instant on the dance floor when she believed Ryan was about to kiss her. She'd longed for his kiss, desired it with an intensity that left her both trembling and frightened. Shouldn't she be thanking Fletcher for ruining the moment? If he hadn't come along, where would another kiss have led them? To more kisses — and more regrets?

In a few short months, they would be separated by more than mere physical distance. Their careers were headed in opposite directions, like a highway that split into two roads snaking off in vastly divergent ways. Where were the walls she'd thrown up around her heart after her parents' deaths to shield herself from the pain of loving and losing someone again? Brutal honesty forced her to acknowledge that those walls had been breached the moment Ryan had kissed her. Or perhaps it was long before that, and she hadn't been aware of it. So much the greater urgency to repair them. Before her heart fully betrayed her. Before she cast a lifetime's hard work and discipline aside and fell foolishly in love with Ryan Maxwell.

Like a phantom invading a troubled dream, Ryan's voice called out to her from the kitchen.

"What would you like to eat?" he asked.

Food was the last thing on her mind. "I don't know," she said. She remembered the cinnamon rolls. "I bought ground coffee and cinnamon rolls at the Coffee Mill yesterday." It seemed years ago that she'd breezed into the market and made her purchases. "We could have that if you want."

"Sounds great."

"The rolls are in the cabinet by the refrigerator." She winced in pain as she shifted her weight to find a more comfortable position on the sofa. "You can heat the rolls in the microwave. The coffee's in the canister on the counter. And the plates and cups are in the cupboard by the sink, the silverware in the drawer by the dishwasher."

"Got it, Kayla."

She heard him whistling. There was the sound of cabinet doors being opened and closed, then the rattle of plates and cups, the ding of the timer on the microwave. Efficient, homey type noises — except for the whistling, which she took as a sign that Ryan was happy puttering around in her kitchen.

Soon he was back in the living room, bearing a tray laden with the rolls, cups of coffee, and a glass of water. He set the tray on an end table beside the sofa, removed one of the cups and a roll on a plate. Then he placed the tray on Kayla's lap. "All right," he said. "It's pill time."

Kayla played along. At least he was teasing her now, and she welcomed it as a sign that maybe he, too, was anxious to put some much-needed levity back into their relationship. "Yes, Dr. Maxwell," she said, making a face at him before she gulped down the huge pink pill he handed her. The spicy scent of the warmed rolls, the nutty aroma of the coffee, stirred her appetite a little. "This smells delicious."

"Glad you think so." Ryan flashed her a grin as he settled himself in the easy chair that was by the sofa.

Though she'd hoped to do justice to the huge roll, she only managed to eat a few small bites. The pain in her ankle had lessened, but the strain of that long night was taking its toll on her. Ryan must have seen that she was fading. He sprang up and took the tray from her lap.

"We have to get you into bed," he whispered, aiding her to her feet.

His nearness, his arm at her waist was suddenly too much. All her fresh resolve threatened to flee, and she knew if she didn't escape him, she was apt to do something foolish. Like throw her arms around his neck and kiss him. "There's no need to fuss over me like a mother hen," she protested, "when anyone can see I'm perfectly capable of walking on my own."

"Is that so?" he challenged, holding her tighter.

She twisted out of his embrace and grasped at a corner of the end table to keep from toppling over. "I'm not a baby," she snapped, "even if you're determined to treat me like one."

He planted his legs apart. "Who said that you were?"

"And . . ." She raised her chin defiantly. "You don't have to act like a martyr, Ryan Maxwell!"

His eyes darkened; his jaw was fixed in a hard line. "I'll take that as a compliment. Before, I was just a fussy mother hen. Now I've been nominated for sainthood."

"I . . . let me go." She squirmed away from him and made her way doggedly across the room. All the while, Ryan's gaze burned at her back.

He didn't come after her, only sarcastically called out, "Don't forget, St. Maxwell's at your service."

Ignoring him, Kayla limped into the bedroom and decisively shut the door. She leaned against the wall, trying to summon enough energy to get herself ready for bed. Finally, she hobbled into the bathroom where she managed to wash her face and brush her teeth. At least she should be glad that her place had a half bath off the living room. That way, she and Ryan wouldn't have to risk facing each other until morning.

With effort, she wriggled out of her clothes and reached for her raggedy nightgown. On second thought, she decided on another, more decent-looking gown of blue cotton. She slipped the gown over her head and removed the comb from her hair, untangling the strands with her fingers. Then she crawled into bed and yanked the covers up to her chin. In the twilight zone between consciousness and sleep, she imagined herself protesting in vain as Ryan scooped her up in his strong arms and carried her toward a storybook castle, its every window shimmering with golden light.

Ryan woke with a start. He sat bolt upright and peered into the semidarkness. He'd had a bad dream of finding Kayla lying helpless and injured on the steps of Timberfrost Lodge, of lifting her in his arms and trying to comfort her. But that wasn't all. He'd also dreamed of holding her close and kissing her.

His eyes finally cleared of sleep, and he blinked. Where was he? Not in his own bed, he realized. A burbling sound drew his attention, and he remembered that he was in Kayla's apartment, bunked down on her couch. The burbling noise came from the filtration system in Angelfish Eve's aquarium.

The dream hadn't been just his subconscious working overtime. Kayla had been injured and he'd come to her aid. The only part that hadn't been true was the part where he'd kissed her. Instead, they'd butted heads and almost had a fight before she'd stalked into her bedroom.

A low groan escaped him as he tried to stretch his legs and they collided with the end of the sofa. He swung his feet onto the floor and put his head in his hands. He'd made a wreck of last night with Kayla, almost let his passion get the better of him. And because of that, she was nursing an injured ankle, and their hopes of winning the pairs title in the Golden Skates appeared to be in greater peril than before.

Ryan forced himself to get up from the sofa. The light from the aquarium threw a strange yellowish cast across a portion of the long living room. He sauntered over to the tank and looked in. Eve was stationed by the door of her new castle.

"Standing watch, are you, Eve?" He tapped his thumb against the glass of the tank. "I'll bet you're worried about Kayla, too." The fish opened and closed her mouth, releasing a stream of bubbles that floated up to the top of the water and broke on the surface.

Ryan consulted his watch by the light. Five o'clock. He'd been asleep for about three hours. It wouldn't be dawn until around seven, and he doubted Kayla would waken before that.

He walked softly to the bedroom door and peeked in. Kayla had left a night light on, and by its dim glow, he could make out her form under the covers of the bed. She made no movement when he opened the door a little wider and crept over to the bed. He just wanted to check on her, to see if she was resting soundly. The sight of her lying there asleep, her lips slightly parted, her hair spread like black silk across the white satin pillowcase, caught at his heart.

He longed to touch her — do more than touch her. He needed to tell her how sorry he was for everything that had happened the night before. Well, not everything, just the part where he'd almost lost control of his senses. Gazing at her now, he realized that nothing had changed. He still wanted to cover her face with his kisses, to take her in his arms and hold her until he saw her eyes darken with love instead of pain.

He dragged himself away from the bed and back to the living room. *Got to get control. It'll be a long day ahead. Warm and cold baths for the ankle. Exercise. Got to keep Kayla's spirits up, too.* Then there was the matter of the club's rehearsal that evening. The kids would be sure to miss Kayla.

Ryan ached with exhaustion, and he knew he needed rest if he was to be of any help to his partner. Scrunching his frame onto the too-short, too-narrow couch, he shut his eyes. But all he saw in his mind was a vision of Kayla sleeping peacefully in her bed. As he lay there in the dark, he wondered how to put a damper on the desire her presence stoked inside of him, threatening to consume every promise he'd ever made to her in his heart.

Kayla woke to the aroma of freshly brewed coffee. For a moment she felt confused. How could she be smelling coffee? She stretched, and the pain that raced through her ankle brought everything back to her.

"Good morning."

Kayla gasped and sat up straight. Ryan stood in the doorway, filling the entrance with his tall, masculine presence. With her own "Good morning," she recalled the unkind things she'd said to him as she'd huffed off to bed.

"How'd you sleep?"

She cleared her throat. "Pretty well. I guess it was the pill." She noted that Ryan's sweater and slacks were rumpled, and that he was in his bare feet. The effect was that he looked more stunningly handsome than he had the night before.

He also looked as if he hadn't shut his eyes the entire night. But he didn't seem to hold anything against her for her cutting remarks. "How did you rest on the sofa?" she asked.

"Well enough." He took a couple of steps into the bedroom. "How's the ankle doing?"

"Hurting some."

"We should start with the warm and cold baths. Then I'll make breakfast."

"No. Really, I'm able to do the baths and make my own breakfast. You need to take care of yourself, too," she said. *Please leave, Ryan — for both our sakes.*

"I am taking care of myself," he replied. He came as far as the end of the bed. "But I intend to head home and change my clothes. Get a shave, too, and pick up the bike. That is, as soon as you show me you can navigate from here to the living room without ending up on the floor with a more serious injury."

The determined glint in his eye told Kayla that it was useless to argue. "You win," she said with a sigh. "There's a basin under the kitchen sink that I use for my hand washing. I can soak the ankle in that." She got out of bed, acutely conscious that Ryan was watching her. "If you'll give me a minute to dress . . ."

Without warning, she began to pitch forward. The pain that cut a jagged path along her ankle must have thrown her off balance. She groped frantically for the nightstand that was beside her bed. Before she could brace herself against the table, Ryan's arm caught her around the waist.

"Careful," he said.

"I'm . . . all right." She was far from all right as Ryan's arm stayed firmly at her waist, his fingers pressed into her flesh through the thin fabric of her gown. Memories of other recent close encounters with him came flooding back, like a tidal wave in her head.

"Kayla . . ."

His voice carried a husky, desperate quality, and she began to feel woozy for reasons that had nothing to do with her ankle. Her hand seemed to have a mind of its own as it came up to stroke the dark shadow of stubble that covered his chin. "You do need a shave," she whispered, suddenly fascinated by the rough feel of his beard against her palm.

"Yes." He looked grim as he seized her hand in an almost painful grip and lowered it to her side. "I'll get the basin ready for your ankle," he said abruptly, turning on his heel.

Why on earth did I have to touch him like that? she asked herself angrily. Her actions had only succeeded in making matters worse between them.

By the time she'd finished washing up and dressing in her jeans skirt and a white sweater, Kayla had managed to regain a measure of inner composure which she tried to assure herself was matched by her outward appearance.

"Mmm. What's that?" she asked, sniffing the air as she limped into the living room.

Ryan glanced over his shoulder from where he stood at the stove. "Just a couple of omelets and home-fried potatoes. I've been told I make a pretty decent omelet." He held up a skillet. "Let's see. Besides half a dozen eggs, I found a potato, an onion, and a green pepper that looked as if it would go belly up if it didn't get eaten soon. I hope you don't mind that I raided your fridge."

Kayla couldn't help smiling. So it seemed her partner was something of a whiz in the kitchen. "Why would I mind when you're making something that smells so delicious?"

"Before we eat, though, your ankle needs to take a dip in the warm water. I set the basin by the end of the sofa. There's a towel beside it."

Kayla sat down on the sofa and removed

the bandage from her ankle. She was relieved to see that there wasn't much swelling at the site of the injury. Waving the socks aloft, she said, "I believe these belong to you, Ryan."

"Not until your ankle's able to stand on its own." He came to join her on the couch. "The omelets and potatoes are keeping hot in the oven. Is the water temp comfy?"

Kayla slipped her foot and ankle into the basin. "Perfect." The warm water gently enveloped her ankle.

"Try your alphabet, and I'll time the four minutes."

She moved her ankle and foot up and down, then sideways. Though the tendons hurt, she was encouraged that she could do the exercise Dr. Quintana had prescribed. She formed an "a" with her toe, then a "b." Sliding a glance at her partner, she said, "Last night you mentioned that you learned how to wrap an injured ankle from Bill. How'd he happen to teach you that particular trick?"

"Well, the first time I sprained my ankle . . ."

Her toe froze mid-letter. "The *first* time?"

Ryan chuckled. "That was when I was

eleven. The second time I was thirteen. I was the original klutz back then."

She surreptitiously regarded his trim, muscular body. It was impossible to imagine he'd ever been a klutz. "So Bill came to your rescue like you came to mine."

He folded his hands together. "I was finishing up a long practice when I lost my balance and fell on my rear. My ankle and foot somehow got caught under me. Luckily, Bill knew just what to do. He whipped off his socks and folded them into a sling."

"I guess we're both indebted to Bill." She wriggled her toes. "How am I doing?"

"Terrific!" Ryan checked his watch. "Time's up."

She lifted her foot out of the water and waited while Ryan exchanged the warm water for cold in the basin. She gritted her teeth when she dipped her foot in the frigid water, but she was determined to do whatever was necessary in order to be back on the ice come Tuesday.

By the end of the twenty minute cycle, Kayla found that she'd become adept at writing the alphabet with her big toe. But her ankle was hurting fiercely. "I think I'd better pop another pain pill."

Ryan took the basin to the kitchen and returned with a mug of coffee. "You're a trouper, Kayla, you know that?"

Her eyes met his. "I would say that makes two of us." They looked at each other for a long moment. Then Ryan suddenly rose from the sofa.

"We'd better eat the omelets or they'll turn to rubber," he said with his back turned to her.

Kayla thought the food was a convenient diversion for avoiding the chemistry that was brewing between them again. She heard the sound of plates clashing together in the kitchen and saw that Ryan was standing with his back and broad shoulders to her, dishing up the food. *He'll make a great husband for some woman one day.*

Now where had *that* notion come from? She almost laughed out loud. The idea of Ryan Maxwell settling into a life of cozy domesticity was about as probable as a heat wave in December on the top of Pikes Peak. *Or as likely as me assuming the role of a dutiful wife and mother,* she thought.

All the recent talk about weddings was putting crazy ideas into her head. After all, Meghan and Scott were newly engaged. Then there was Estelle's ill-timed observation about Ryan resembling a groom about to be wed. *Not to mention the kiss we shared in the parking lot.* Or the tension that been simmering in the air ever since, like water ready to boil on a red-hot stove.

As she saw Ryan coming with the plates of food, she told herself that the only thing that mattered was their shared dream of winning the Golden Skates and becoming world champions. If they were half the troupers they claimed to be, then they should be able to set any mutual attraction aside and pour every ounce of their energies into achieving that dream. Their separate plans for the future, their very survival as a team now demanded that much of them.

Chapter Eleven

The sound of the front door opening roused Kayla from where she was nestled on the sofa. Through sleep-blurred eyes, she saw Ryan coming across the room, his stationary bicycle in tow. Her watch told her she'd slept a couple of hours.

"Where do you want the bike?" he asked.

"Maybe . . . by the window," she said, stifling a yawn. She hobbled after him and watched him set up the bike.

"Do you feel like going a mile or so?" he said.

"Of course. How else am I going to work off that wood-chopper's breakfast you fed me?"

His eyes crinkled with amusement. "I'll help you on."

Before she knew what was happening, his hands circled her waist and lifted her onto the cycle. When he reached over to zero out the odometer, the scent of his cologne teased her nostrils, and she noticed that he no longer had a five-o'clock shadow.

"There, you're all set," he said.

"Hmmm? Oh, yes, all set."

He looked around, as if he were uncertain of what to do next. "Got any new puzzles?" he asked.

"The Labyrinth." She pulled her gaze away from his cleanly shaven jaw. "Top shelf, on the right," she added.

Ryan retrieved the puzzle and sat down cross-legged on the floor near the bike. "Looks like a good challenge," he said, dumping the puzzle pieces onto the carpet.

Kayla pedaled while her partner began to sort through the pieces of the Labyrinth. Apparently the pain pill she'd taken with breakfast was still doing its job. The discomfort in her ankle was tolerable, and she had a stunning view of Pikes Peak out the window. But her eyes kept returning to the sight of her partner's bowed, tousled head, and as soon as the odometer clicked past a mile, she slid off the bike and onto the floor beside Ryan.

They worked together on the Labyrinth for a while. Ryan teased her whenever she mismatched puzzle pieces, and she laughed, deceiving herself into thinking that it was just like old times.

Ryan stretched his legs in front of him. "We'll have to finish this up tomorrow. The club's got rehearsal this evening, so I'm afraid you'll be on your own then."

She'd completely forgotten about rehearsal. "Couldn't I go with you — just to watch?"

"Nope." He regarded her with a look of mock sternness. "I know you. If you set one foot in the arena, next thing you'll be lacing up your skates. How about some lunch while your ankle's taking a dip in the basin? I spotted a couple of cans of tuna in the cupboard last night."

After she'd eaten and exercised her ankle in the warm and cold baths, Kayla felt ready for another pain pill.

"Another nap wouldn't hurt either," Ryan suggested, and she had to reluctantly agree.

No sooner had she made herself comfortable on the bed than the phone rang in the living room. She heard Ryan answer the call. With the door to her bedroom halfway closed, she could catch only bits and pieces of Ryan's end of the conversation. She heard just enough to know the call had to be from Eve.

Curiosity won out over sleepiness. She

crept over to the door and opened it a crack wider. But Ryan was already placing the receiver back in its cradle.

He regarded her from where he sat slouched on the sofa. "That was a short snooze."

"Do you think I'd be sleeping like a log while you're fending off Eve's questions?" She plopped down on the opposite end of the couch. "How's Carl?"

"Improving. He's been moved out of intensive care."

"That's encouraging news. What did you tell Eve about us?"

He took the phone again and uncoiled the cord that had somehow gotten twisted. "That we're doing okay."

"Do you think she believed you?"

Ryan shrugged. "She didn't quiz me, didn't even ask why I was answering your phone for you." He set the phone back in its place. "A cousin of Carl's is driving in tomorrow to help out Lila when Carl comes home from the hospital. Eve's already booked a flight home. She'll be in on Wednesday, she said."

"And by then I'll be back on the ice."

He didn't respond to the remark, just stared at his feet. "Ryan." He glanced up. "Are we okay?"

The question hung in the air between them. He squared his shoulders. "Why shouldn't we be? Your ankle's getting better. We'll be a team again by Tuesday. We'll . . ."

"I'm talking about what's happening between us off the ice." His scowl told her she'd hit a sensitive spot. A voice inside her head warned her to stop, but she had to know if he truly believed the things he was saying to her. "I'm talking about last night — and about when we kissed outside Estelle's," she said.

Ryan gazed stone-faced at the wall. It was a long time before he spoke. "What happened last night — and at Estelle's — is best forgotten," he said in a quietly controlled voice. "We lost our heads a couple of times, forgot who we were and where we're going."

"So you honestly think it's as simple as that, Ryan?"

"Yes."

The curtness of his response, his defensive stance, made her prickle with irritation. But his body language also made her believe that his experience with his former partner had caused him to throw up walls around his heart, too. Or maybe, she thought with fresh exasperation, he was so used to passing out kisses that one or two tossed her way really was no big deal to him. Yet deep inside she doubted the validity of her own reasoning. Ryan had always treated her with the greatest respect. Why would he suddenly do any less than that now, with their partnership nearing an end? Still, it was obvious to her that he had no intention of carrying the conversation further. And that left her with no choice but to tell him coldly, "Then I'll see you at the arena on Tuesday morning."

Ryan jerked to his feet. "No. I'm coming over in the morning and we're going for a walk in Prospect Park."

His dogged insistence frayed her patience. "Don't trouble yourself, Ryan Maxwell," she retorted, glaring at him.

"Don't worry," he growled, "I'm not." He studied her through narrowed eyes. "It's my fault you fell at the lodge. Now I'm taking care of you." His little speech concluded, he grabbed his jacket and strode out the door.

Long after Ryan had slammed the door closed behind him, Kayla sat on the sofa, trying to make sense out of their latest spat — and her own conflicting feelings. A part of her was rankled by his show of protective concern; another part was more pleased than she cared to admit.

She hugged a plump throw pillow against her stomach and thought that she couldn't recall a time when she'd felt so exhausted after doing nothing but pedal a stationary bicycle one mile. Finally, she lay down on the couch, tucked the pillow under her head, and drifted into a troubled sleep.

Kayla wakened with a startled cry. She noticed she was trembling as she pushed herself into a sitting position. She'd been dreaming about her natural parents, about that vividly sunny March day when the patrol car had pulled up in front of her coach's house where she'd been staying while her parents were away on business in New York.

In the nightmare, she'd relived it all again — the subdued tone of the highway patrolman who was talking to Cleo in the living room while Sharon kept Kayla occupied in the kitchen. Then the moment when Cleo had joined them at the kitchen table and taken Kayla's small hands between his two large ones. With tears welling in his eyes, he'd broken the news about the terrible accident in which her father had lost control of their car on a rain-slicked road.

Why had the dream come back to haunt her now? Tears trickled down her face, and she began to weep in earnest. Sobs wracked her body, leaving her gasping for breath. She'd thought she'd been through with mourning long ago. But her sorrow was so fresh and raw that she felt as if she were grieving over the death of her parents for the first time.

Kayla rose from the sofa and limped to the window. The late-afternoon sun was already dropping behind the Peak. Its fading rays ringed the snowy cap of the mountain with a glorious golden halo. A lone star, faintly visible in the darkening sky, winked at Kayla.

Starlight, star bright, first star I see tonight . . . Kayla heard from the past the gentle voice of her mother, softly teaching her the simple, familiar rhyme. *What should I wish for now?* she wondered. An exciting career as a professional singles skater? Fame and fortune with a prestigious touring company?

She remembered Ryan's smiling face and the cheerful sound of his whistling as he puttered about in her kitchen. A fresh tear slid down her cheek, and suddenly her wishes and dreams for the future seemed as hollow and empty as her heart at that moment.

Seven sad pairs of eyes stared up at Ryan. He'd just told the club members about Kayla's injury. "She'll be fine," he said, wondering if he sounded convincing.

"I'm going to miss her."

"We'll all miss her, Shelly." He missed her like crazy right that minute. He was shaken up by their latest argument, and it had taken all his willpower not to march back into her apartment and plead for her forgiveness. He longed to make good on his promise to take care of her — not just for now, but for keeps.

"I've been practicing my Salchow," Shelly went on. Her lower lip curled in disappointment, "I wanted to show her."

"I know she's anxious to see your jump." Ryan put his arm around the girl. "Kayla will be back on Tuesday. That's only a couple more days, you know."

"My brother sprained his ankle once," Nathan announced. "He was on crutches for six weeks. I used to steal one of the crutches and we'd have sword fights with 'em." He put his right arm behind his back and held his other arm out straight, making thrusts with it as if he were wielding a make-believe sword.

Petey brightened. "Wow! Will Kayla have'ta skate with crutches?"

"That's silly, Petey," Shelly said with a toss of her long curls. "Kayla doesn't need crutches because she's got Ryan."

Ryan felt like smiling for the first time in hours. But the kids were completely serious.

"That's right," Gina agreed. "If Kayla starts to fall, Ryan'll just put his arms around her like this . . ." She grabbed hold of Nathan in an obvious attempt to demonstrate the technique, but he managed to squirm away. The girl sighed. "Well, Ryan will catch her. Won't you?"

His smile faded. "That's right, Gina." He looked over the heads of the seven youngsters clustered around him. If the kids only knew. The fact was that now when he took Kayla in his arms, he wanted to do far more than keep her from falling.

His gaze connected with Petey's. The boy looked disappointed. No doubt Petey had hoped to see Kayla tooling around the rink on crutches. Ryan mussed the boy's hair. At the same time, he spotted Meghan and Scott speeding across the ice in his direction.

"Okay," he said, clapping his hands. "Let's have a fifteen-minute warm-up." At the familiar signal, the club members zipped in seven different directions.

Meghan waved, then circled around to hook up with Shelly. *Great,* thought Ryan. *The girl could use some extra encouragement.* Scott came on to meet him at the boards.

"How's Kayla? You taking good care of her?" Scott reached out and high-fived Nathan as the boy skated past.

Ryan regarded his friend. "Have to, Scott. She's my partner. Her ankle's coming along," he added. "She'll be back on Tuesday."

"What about you, bud?" Scott smoothed a hand over the top of his brown hair. "Are you doing all right?"

"Sure. All Kayla and I have to do is get our program to click, and we'll be set."

"Set for what?"

"To win the Golden Skates — what else?"

"Have you considered that the problem might be more what's going on with you and Kayla as a man and a woman instead of as partners?"

Ryan fell silent, feigning a deep interest in the jump Shelly was demonstrating for Meghan. "The truth is," he said in a voice that sounded strangely foreign to his ears,

"I'm falling in love with Kayla." He faced Scott. "I guess I just came to fully realize it last night."

"And falling in love is a problem?"

"A problem?" Ryan gave a bitter laugh. "It's an impossibility."

"But it's happened anyway."

"Yeah." Ryan impatiently flicked a piece of lint off his warm-up suit. "But I'm going to get it under control. After Worlds, Kayla'll be joining a tour, and I'll be packing up and heading out to New York. You know that Bill's got a job waiting for me."

"Haven't you ever heard of a long-distance love affair?"

"What're you trying to do? Play devil's advocate?"

Scott chuckled. "Not at all. It's a practical thing. You love Kayla. From what I can tell, it's about as plain as the nose on your face that she loves you, too. She's turning pro. You're turning to coaching. It may not be ideal, but lots of people who're in love have separate careers these days. Remember, bud, there are planes and trains and telephones."

Ryan set his jaw. "It wouldn't work for Kayla and me."

"Why not?"

Why not? It was a good question, wasn't it? "I couldn't live like that. I don't think she could, either."

"How can you be so certain?"

He thought about it. Suddenly, deep inside, he knew why he was so certain. "Because my father couldn't. And I can't be sure that I'm not my father's son."

Scott put his hand on Ryan's shoulder. "What do you mean by that?" he asked quietly.

"My parents had a commuter-type marriage. My father was a salesman, traveled all over the country. After eleven years of marriage and a kid — me — he left Mom high and dry for a woman fifteen years younger. Apparently, that wasn't the first time he'd cheated on Mom. His excuse was that life on the road was just too lonely, the temptations too great."

"I'm sorry. I knew your mother died a few years ago, but you never told me how her marriage ended."

Ryan forced a smile. "Mom and I managed to make it through on our own — no thanks to my father."

"You sure did, bud." Scott paused. "But I think you're being unfair to yourself. Your father made a choice — a bad one. That doesn't mean you would make that same kind of choice."

"I'd say I've already got a pretty good head start," he countered. "A different girlfriend every few months, an address book stocked with phone numbers and addresses of willing and eager women from any city you can name."

"And how many of those willing and eager women have you asked out on a date in the past couple of years?"

Ryan was loath to admit that the answer was close to zilch.

Scott grinned. "I thought so. I don't mean to be presumptuous here, Ryan, but it seems obvious to me that you're still beating yourself up for what happened between you and Gillian, for decisions that Gillian made. You've been running scared, trying to persuade yourself that you need to be dating every beautiful female in sight because you've been afraid of owning up to your love for Kayla."

A painful feeling of tightness gripped Ryan's insides. "I couldn't stand myself if I made the same mistakes with Kayla that I made with Gillian," he gritted out through clenched teeth. "If I messed up Kayla's future."

"Hey, take it easy, Ryan." Scott patted him on the arm. "Love can be an amazing thing. It can sometimes almost work miracles."

Ryan stared down at his skates. "It would take a miracle to heal this bum knee of mine." Or to shake those old demons from his past that warned him the only way he could ever show his love for Kayla was to let her go. He was about to tell Scott as much when Meghan's approach cut him short. He remembered he had a rehearsal to run.

"Crystal Palace Club members," he called out with fake enthusiasm, "it's show time!"

Despite his divided state of mind, Ryan was satisfied with the evening's rehearsal. To their credit, the kids were on their best behavior, and with the exception of Petey taking a fall on his toe loop, only a few minor errors marred the smoothness of the production number. Shelly nailed her Salchow, and the conga line finale came off with just a couple of hitches.

Ryan had Shelly trade places with Gina in the line. Then they went through the finale again. *Better,* he thought. Shelly was the stronger skater of the two; she added stability to the middle of the line where it was needed most.

When the last notes of the music faded,

Ryan cupped his hands and yelled, "That's a wrap." Seven faces beamed at him. The girls gave way to giggles, as usual. He waved the kids off and went to thank Meghan for the help she'd given Shelly.

"I know how special Shelly is to Kayla," she said, wiping a bead of perspiration from her upper lip. "I was thinking that if you and Scotty don't need me at rehearsal tomorrow night, I'd like to spend some time with Kayla. I want her opinion on some pictures of wedding and bridesmaid dresses."

Ryan slanted his gaze away from Meghan. "I imagine Kayla would like that." He waited at the boards until Scott returned. Then he took off toward the exit.

He was accosted under the exit sign by Shelly and Nathan. Turning, he saw the other members of the club were there, too.

"We want to give Kayla a card so she'll feel better."

"That's a great idea, Shelly." He gathered the kids into a circle around him.

"We want to make the card ourselves," Gina volunteered. "Nathan draws real good, so he can do the cover. We thought a picture of you and Kayla skating would be cool."

Ryan looked at Nathan. "Is that all right with you?"

"Yeah." He grinned shyly. "I'll do it tonight."

"Tomorrow we'll all sign our names," Petey chimed in.

Ryan was touched by the kids' concern. "I'll make a delivery of the card to Kayla after rehearsal," he said.

The members of the club nodded in unison. Then they filed out, and Ryan found himself alone. He looked around. Scott and Meghan were gone. No one else was on the ice but him. Saturday nights were always quiet at the arena unless there was a competition or exhibition scheduled.

Almost without conscious thought, Ryan began to circle the ice. The rink could be a lonely place for a skater practicing by himself. Tonight it seemed to Ryan as if the temperature in the place had been adjusted down a few notches. But he reasoned that his apartment could be awfully cold and lonely, too.

The idea of going home to his empty efficiency held no appeal to Ryan. Was it because he missed Kayla — missed her with an ache that wouldn't quit? He told himself he'd better get used to cold and lonely because there'd be enough nights like this ahead — nights and days and years that stretched on and on in his mind like a long mountain highway that had no end.

His conversation with Scott replayed over in his head. He respected his buddy's practical wisdom, his sage advice. But that didn't change anything. Not the fact that he was deep in the last days of his skating career. Not his unshakable conviction that emotionally he couldn't handle a long-distance love affair with Kayla. Not his stubborn determination that she have her very best shot at the career she deserved.

Ryan skated lap after lap. With each lap he went faster, as if he were chasing a dream that lay just out of his grasp. The dream of holding Kayla in his arms, off the ice as well as on, not for a few more months, but forever.

He launched himself with a vengeance into a double Lutz. No sooner had his feet touched the ice than he threw himself into a triple axel, then another double Lutz. He sped around the perimeter of the ice as if he were eighteen again until his throbbing knee reminded him that he was on the downhill side of twenty-eight. Finally, he made himself slow to a stop at the boards.

Spent, he stood there, half doubled over, gulping air. It was useless. No matter how fast he skated, how hard he pushed, he couldn't escape the dream that haunted him.

Chapter Twelve

"So what do you think of Marty's suggestion?"

Kayla glanced over at her partner who sat next to her on a bench by Prospect Lake. She reached in the paper bag that lay between them and withdrew a handful of popcorn. "You mean about changing our triple toe loop to a Lutz and adding another triple Salchow?" She tossed the popcorn to a fat gray pigeon that had been marching back and forth in front of the bench. The bird greedily gobbled down the white puffy kernels.

"Yes. Have you come to any conclusions?" Ryan stared at the lake, his hands stuffed in the pockets of his tan windbreaker.

Since he'd come for her that morning, he'd said little except to tell her he was pleased that her ankle was doing better and to say the previous night's rehearsal had gone well and that the kids had missed her. All the while Kayla longed for a way to bridge the silence that had risen like a wall between them as soon as they'd left her apartment for the park.

When he'd suggested that they sit on the park bench, she hadn't objected. He'd commented on how changeable the weather had been lately; she'd remarked that the ski season would soon be in full swing in the mountains. He'd wondered whether powder conditions would be better this year in Vail or at Copper Mountain. They both loved to ski and, in past winters, had occasionally taken off with a group of other local skaters for a day on the slopes. Now those carefree times seemed gone forever, and Kayla felt as if she were engaged in a careful dance with Ryan, both of them clumsily grasping at verbal straws while waltzing around the issue that loomed like a closed gate in front of them — their feelings for each other.

"Kayla?"

Her mind jolted back to his question. "I suppose Marty's right. The change would punch up our program some." She tried to gauge his reaction, but he kept his gaze fixed on the lake, and so she stared out over the choppy water, too. A chill breeze raised ripples on the surface and sent them scudding toward the shoreline. "Or don't you agree?"

"I agree."

Why are we discussing toe loops and Salchows when we need to be talking about what's happening between us? The sudden touch of his fingers on her cheek checked the breath in her throat, and she turned to find him watching her.

The expression in his eyes was unreadable, but his fingers were gentle as they smoothed back wisps of her hair that the wind had displaced.

Abruptly, he withdrew his hand. "We'd better take that walk," he said.

In silence they began to stroll along a path that skirted the lake. Near the shore, an older couple were throwing cubes of bread to a flock of Canada geese that was gathered around them. The man bent forward and rested his hand on the woman's arm. Whatever he said to her was lost on the wind, but her laughing response was carried over the water to Kayla. It seemed to Kayla that everywhere she went these days, she saw couples happily in love.

"Look, Kayla."

She followed her partner's gaze to a tall

pine tree beside the path. "What? I don't see anything?"

"A woodpecker." Ryan pointed. "He's perched on the next-to-the-lowest branch."

She finally spotted the redheaded bird. "Do you suppose he's as curious about us as we are of him?"

"I used to be a member of Birdwatchers-International, you know."

"You're kidding. You never told me that before." She couldn't picture anything less likely than the image of her partner tramping through the woods ferreting out nuthatches and chickadees with a pair of binoculars.

He smiled. "I'm not kidding. When I was eleven years old, my mom joined the group." The smile disappeared from his face. "It was a few months after the divorce. I think she was trying to find something . . . some activity that we could do together to kind of make up for Dad checking out of our lives."

There was a lingering touch of bitterness in his voice, a trace of sadness that Kayla had heard before on the rare occasion when he broached the subject of his parents' divorce and his father's disappearance from his life. "I hope you have happy memories of those times with your mother," she said quietly.

He pushed his hands into his jacket pockets. "I do," he said. "Not that I didn't buck the idea at first. I thought bird-watching was sissy stuff. Besides, I had enough teasing from the kids at school about my skating. But that was before I learned that my coach was a confirmed bird-watcher."

"You mean Bill?"

Amusement flickered in Ryan's eyes. "He and Margie used to belong to the group, until he got real involved in his coaching duties and had to give up the hobby for a while. But when he found out that Mom and I were hitting the trails with our swamp waders and binoculars, he and Margie joined up again. After that, they always accompanied Mom and me." He peered up at the sky. "We used to take our backpacks and camp out. I don't think I've ever seen so many stars since as I saw in the summer sky those nights we spent together."

Ryan fell silent, and as they moved on, Kayla thought about the things he'd told her. She better understood his deep affection for Bill. The coach had been a father figure to Ryan after his natural dad had taken his leave — much the same as Cleo and Sharon had been loving parents to her after the loss of her mother and father. But there was a critical difference. His father's act of abandonment had been a conscious decision, one that she suspected had hurt Ryan in ways he didn't realize, even to this day. She ached for him, longed to reach out to him and offer a comforting word or touch. But she feared that if she did, he would only withdraw from her, and she didn't want to risk destroying the new fragile bond of camaraderie they shared. Casting a glance his way, she saw that he was again favoring his knee.

"Is your knee bothering you?" she ventured asking.

He shrugged. "A little. I did a few jumps last night after rehearsal. Maybe one too many."

"We don't have to walk, Ryan. I've got the bike at home." Why should he risk aggravating the knee? "We didn't need to come to the park today."

All at once he ground to a stop and grasped her by the shoulders. "I told you we were going to take a walk around the lake — and that's what we're doing," he said tersely.

His hands held her possessively, but his countenance looked as bleak as a bare mountaintop in storm, and when she twisted away from him, he let her go without a protest.

The bond of camaraderie was gone, replaced by a stubborn silence. They completed their hike and rode back to Kayla's apartment without exchanging so much as a banal comment about the weather.

By the time Ryan swung the BMW into a vacant parking space in the lot of her building, Kayla had decided that the only way to preserve her sanity was to firmly tell Ryan that she wanted to spend the afternoon alone. And if he persisted in his role of caregiver, she would just as persistently tell him she was firing him from the job.

She had no chance to say anything. Despite his lame knee, Ryan got out of the car with surprising dexterity and strode around to her side. He opened the door for her. Then he shoved his hands back in his pockets and kept them there as he walked her up to the entrance of her building.

"If you'll be okay for a while, I'll be heading home," he said, gazing at the wall. His words echoed in the tiny foyer.

"How many times do I have to tell you that I can take care of myself?" she huffed. A chill spread slowly through her blood and seeped into her bones.

His expression was impassive, and she imagined they must look like two wary strangers who were meeting for the first time — and didn't like what they saw.

"See you after rehearsal then," he said.

Don't bother. She bit back the words and said nothing at all. In an instant he was gone, and she stood watching the door swing shut after him.

"I sort of like this one. What do you think?"

"What?" Kayla blinked. Her eyes slowly focused on the picture of a wedding gown lavishly trimmed in lace. "Oh, yes, that would look just perfect on you, Meghan."

"Thanks, but . . ." Meghan took the catalog from Kayla's lap and put it aside. "Your mind's a million miles away. Do you want to talk about what's bothering you? Or will I have to pry it out of you?"

Kayla averted her eyes. The stationary bike came into her line of vision, and she recalled the firm way Ryan's hands had circled her waist to place her on the seat. Those same capable hands had lifted her in the air countless times on the ice, but never before had she been so conscious of their strength, their ability to both soothe and entice her. Nor had she ever been so aware of their owner's ability to rankle her one moment and kindle the flames of love the next.

"So that's it," Meghan went on. "You've finally come to your senses and realized that you're in love with Ryan."

Kayla met her friend's clear blue gaze. "Falling in love doesn't fit in with my plans for the future."

Meghan grinned. "Since when does falling in love fit in with most people's plans?"

Ignoring the question, Kayla glanced at the bridal magazines and catalogs stacked in her friend's lap. *Love. Marriage. Children. Happily-ever-afters.* They were words she'd never considered applying to herself. Yet all at once they seemed to strike a strange accord in her heart — one that promised to derail every hard-earned dream she'd ever nurtured.

"Face it," Meghan was saying. "You and Ryan were made for each other. I knew something was up when I started to notice the longing looks flying between the two of you. Not to mention the little spats, of course. But the clincher was the party."

Kayla's stomach did a turn. "What do you mean?"

"Nothing except for the way he held you

while you were dancing, so tenderly possessive and dreamy-eyed. Then when you hurt your ankle, he went absolutely pale."

"He was worried about me, that's all." Kayla rose from the sofa and paced toward the kitchen as quickly as her injured ankle would allow. She didn't want to hear any more reasons why Meghan was certain that Quinn and Maxwell were a love match. "I've got cookies," she said, turning to a cupboard where she retrieved an unopened package of Oreos. "And there's coffee that I made a couple of hours ago. I can warm it up. Or I have peppermint and regular —"

A sharp knock at the door interrupted her recitation. "Tea," she muttered as she went to open the door.

Ryan regarded her uneasily from across the threshold. His arms were loaded with small sacks.

"Hi," she said, feeling much too warm.

"Hi." He looked past her into the living room.

"Meghan's here," she said unnecessarily.

"No, I'm just leaving."

Kayla discovered that her friend was standing right behind her, bridal magazines and catalogs bundled in her arms.

"Excuse me," Meghan said, with a smile

at Ryan, "I'm on my way to meet Scotty." She stepped past Kayla into the hallway. "See you two tomorrow," she called back.

"Are you going to invite me in or do you want to eat your fajitas and guacamole in the hall?"

The flush in Kayla's cheeks deepened as she motioned for him to come in. "Is that what you have in the sacks? Mexican food?" she asked, following him to the dining table.

Ryan set his load on the table and shrugged out of his jacket. "Some of them." He laid his jacket on a chair. "This is from the club members." He handed her an envelope.

She noted the pleased expression on his face. Turning the envelope over in her hands, she saw her name printed crookedly on one side.

"Petey's handiwork," Ryan said. "Go ahead, see what's inside."

Kayla pulled a folded piece of white construction paper from the envelope. "Oh, look . . ." A catch came into her throat when she saw the drawing of herself and Ryan on skates. He had his arm around her. "It's a wonderful picture."

"Nathan drew it."

Across the top of the card was printed the

message, *We hope your ankle gets better soon! We miss you!! P.S. Petey thought you would have to skate on crutches, but I told him that was silly.* Inside the card were the signatures of the seven club members as well as her partner's and Meghan's and Scott's. "How sweet . . ."

"Shelly composed the message."

Kayla smiled at her partner over the card. "Skate on crutches?" she said, her heart warmed by the kids' thoughtfulness.

He grinned as he took the card from her hands and propped it up on the table where she could admire it.

But her attention was more on her partner than on the card. *You two were made for each other. . . .* Meghan's words reeled through her mind. "Did you say something about fajitas?" she asked, looking away.

"Yep. Casa Iguana's specialty."

She started for the kitchen. "I'll get the plates."

"Wait."

She turned around. He was lifting another container out of a bag. Her eyes widened when she saw a live angelfish swimming around in the clear plastic box.

Ryan chuckled. "Don't worry. He won't end up in our fajitas. I bought him for Eve."

"Oh . . ." Kayla felt at a loss for words.

"Why don't we introduce Eve to her new companion."

Kayla watched as Ryan released the fish into the aquarium. Eve floated gracefully past the handsome new arrival as if he didn't exist and headed for the surface of the tank where she blew out a stream of bubbles. Meanwhile, the male fish began to swim toward the castle.

As if an alarm had sounded, Eve darted to the castle and stationed herself at the front door, blocking the intruder's entrance.

"Not a very cordial welcome, I'm afraid," Kayla remarked. "You're sure he *is* a he?"

"If Phil, the owner of the Fish Emporium, is to be believed."

"That's where you bought Eve, too, wasn't it?"

"Yes."

"Did you pick him at random?"

Ryan stepped behind her. His hands came to rest lightly on her shoulders while, in the tank, Eve and the male fish were eyeing each other.

"Not exactly," he said. "When I told Phil what I was looking for, he showed me this little guy, said the fish had lost his mate.

They usually come in matched pairs."

"I didn't know that."

"According to Phil, it's the most ideal arrangement."

"Really?" Kayla tilted her head to glance at Ryan. His breath warmed her cheek, and his nearness warmed her in ways that set her heart pounding.

He smiled. "Uh-huh. Another thing I learned from Phil. The fish that's left behind might never find another suitable match. In other cases it works out well and he and his new mate swim happily off into the sunset together." His expression turned somber. "It's a gamble, Kayla," he said softly.

"Sometimes we have to take chances," she said almost to herself.

"Yes." Ryan whispered the word in her ear as he turned her around.

Her pulse quickened as his gaze roved over her face and came to rest on her mouth. In the next instant she found herself locked in his arms and his lips were possessing hers with all the poignancy of a homecoming. Her lips parted willingly under the tender assault of his mouth. She wrapped her arms around his neck, urging him closer until there was no space left between them at all. Clinging to her partner, she wondered how they could have deprived themselves for so long of the ecstasy of this moment.

He broke the kiss with a ragged gasp. "Kayla . . ." His eyes were suffused with passion, and she shivered at the unspoken questions she read in them.

"For so long I've needed —" he began, cradling her in his arms.

She pressed her fingers to his lips, not wanting explanations, not wanting to think beyond that moment or of anything at all but of her desire for him to kiss her again.

"To hold you, to . . ." he whispered against her fingertips.

"Shh."

Kayla collapsed against him. Her hands clutched at the rough folds of his sweater, roamed over the hard strength of his shoulders. His muscles rippled enticingly beneath her fingers as he pulled her closer, closer until she could barely draw a breath. His hands explored the planes of her back, the hollow of her spine. Intoxicated by his touch, she stroked the column of his neck, laced her fingers in his hair. A rush of heady warmth surged through her when she felt his heart thundering next to hers.

Leaning back, she said with her eyes what she couldn't say aloud. *I love you. I need you.* Words torn from her heart, a silent confession that she could no longer deny.

His gaze told her that he loved her, too. Or did she only imagine it? Shutting out the fear and uncertainty that automatically rose inside her, she gave her lips up to his, returning his kiss with a fervor that matched his own.

From somewhere came a ringing sound, an alarm that Kayla knew she should heed. But it wasn't until Ryan pulled away that she became conscious the ringing wasn't in her head. "The phone," she gasped. Then foggily she remembered that her answering machine was turned on. "Forget it," she said and watched as his mouthed quirked into a lazy smile.

"I will," he whispered, tracing the line of her cheek and jaw with his finger.

For a time there was only the soft sound of their kisses, the intruding noise of the phone. The answering machine clicked on and Kayla's voice told the caller to please leave a message.

"Hi, Kayla. It's Hamil here."

Kayla froze as Ryan tore his mouth from hers. Their eyes met and held; then he slowly put her at arm's length.

"Disappointed I didn't catch you."

Hamil's rich baritone voice seemed to fill the room.

A sick feeling clutched at Kayla's stomach. *This can't be happening.* She jumped up from the sofa and frantically reached out to stop the answering machine. Her trembling fingers fell short of the cutoff button.

". . . luckily I'll be in the Springs the twenty-fourth and twenty-fifth," Hamil droned on. "Why don't we plan on combining a little business with a whole lot of pleasure while I'm in town? I'll call again soon." There was a click, then silence.

Numbness spread through Kayla as she looked across the room at Ryan. He was snatching up his jacket from the chair.

"I'd better be going." He spared her the briefest of glances.

"No, Ryan, don't." She hobbled toward him. "The food. You . . . we haven't eaten," she stammered.

"I'm not hungry," he said with a finality that chilled her as thoroughly as his kisses had warmed her.

A thousand emotions tore at Kayla's heart as she watched Ryan walk out the door. She wanted to call him back, run after him, tell him that Hamil Brookings meant nothing to her, that it was him —

Ryan Maxwell — that she loved.

No, she told herself. *Let him go.* Whatever thoughts she'd entertained of marriage and children, of happily ever after's with Ryan were just that — fanciful thoughts. They had no future together. He had been right, after all, when he'd said they had to forget what had happened between them.

She must force the remembrance of his tender embrace, his hot, sweet kisses to retreat into some dark recess until the memory of them flickered and died like a fire doused by winter rains. But it seemed impossible that she could forget when everywhere she looked she was reminded of his genuine concern for her. And when the exquisite taste of him lingered on her lips, making her long to be held in his arms forever.

Chapter Thirteen

Ryan paced. Back and forth, back and forth, he must've completed a dozen laps around the L-shaped room he called home. Pausing, he looked down at the rumpled sheets of his bed. He'd left it unmade since morning with the notion he'd want to dive under the covers the minute he got home that night.

He laughed at the idea. He knew if he shut his eyes, all he would see behind those closed lids was Kayla. And all he'd want to do was leap out of bed, hop into his car, drive at a reckless rate of speed back to her apartment, and sweep her up in his arms. It was what he wanted to do at that very moment.

Ryan stopped in front of the large window that took up almost half of one wall of the room. He switched off the lamp and yanked open the vertical blinds. Moonlight streamed through the window and spilled onto the carpet.

"Fickle Colorado weather," he muttered, gazing at the heavens. When he'd left Kayla's apartment a couple of hours ago, it was flurrying snow and the moon was hidden by a thick bank of clouds. Now stars were twinkling across a clear sky. Only the wailing of the wind and the naked limbs of the trees shaking in the gale kept Ryan from believing that it was a balmy summer's night.

It might be freezing outside, but it's hot as a July day in here, he thought, beginning to pace again. The problem had nothing to do with the setting on the thermostat on the wall by his bed. His need to see Kayla, to tell her just what she meant to him, threatened to overtake him like a fast-moving fire. He'd been on the verge of breaking down, confessing his true feelings to her, when Brookings called. The timing couldn't have been better, he told himself, flopping onto the bed. Regardless of how much it hurt him to think that she might still be dating the agent, Brookings's call had hurled him back to reality. He'd needed that shock. He'd veered badly off track lately. All that talk about getting his emotions under control had been so much hot air. The only choice left to him now was to set his sights firmly on the goals he'd laid out for himself years ago.

Ryan pushed himself up from the bed, moaning with the pain that sliced through his knee and down his shinbone. Walking at a snail's pace, he went over to the window and flung it open. An arctic blast of wind bit at his face. He inhaled deeply of the frigid air. He felt hollow inside, as if his heart had been ripped from his chest and all that was left was empty space. Thoughts of the rolling foothills of upstate New York and of the village of Winding River rushed into his mind. It'd be cold there, too, the ground covered with snow. He missed those gentle hills; he missed winter up north. But would he find peace there?

Checking his watch by the light of the moon, he saw it was just after ten — midnight, Eastern Time. Once Bill had told him that he rarely turned in until one or two in the morning. So it wasn't too late for a call to Winding River.

Ryan slammed the window shut and went to the phone. He quickly dialed the number he knew from memory. On the fourth ring, he heard the click of the receiver, soft music in the background.

"Brenner residence."

"Hello, Bill?"

"Ryan! This is a surprise. How are you?"

Ryan could hear the smile in Bill's voice. "Fine." *Liar.*

"How're things in Colorado? You've got a competition coming up next week, haven't you?"

"The Golden Skates."

"You and Kayla ready for another win, son?"

A lump like a goose egg rose in Ryan's throat. His affection for Bill ran as clear and deep as the big river that ran alongside the town where the coach had established his rink twenty-five years ago. He couldn't tell Bill another lie. "We've had some trouble with our practices. But we're hoping to pull off the competition."

There was a pause on the coach's end. "That happens. You staying healthy out there?"

"The knee's been giving me grief the past couple of weeks. With any luck, though, it should hold up okay." *A* lot *of luck,* thought Ryan morosely.

"Well, you want to baby it along, take care of yourself. And Kayla. She's a fine young lady. Courageous. And beautiful, too. A true champion."

"I know." *Bill, you're not making things any easier for me.*

"If there's anything I can do for you, son — for the two of you — all you have to do is ask."

"I appreciate that. Actually, I've been doing a lot of thinking about the coaching job."

"You'd like more time, Ryan? I have no problem with that. If you and Kayla want to join a tour, it's fine by me. One year, two, five. It doesn't matter."

Ryan swallowed hard. "No, it's not that. With the knee the way it is, I won't be joining a tour. Kayla'll be turning pro soon, so I thought I'd tie up loose ends here right after Worlds and head out for Winding River. I need to be earning a steady paycheck."

"You sure, son?" Bill said in a quiet voice.

What else would I do? Ryan almost asked. *Follow Kayla on tour, from city to city, living off of her income?* No self-respecting man could do that to the woman he loved.

He clasped the receiver so tight his hand began to shake. "Yeah, I'm sure, Bill. Real sure."

"I've got to get out of this apartment — or go mad," Kayla muttered to herself as she peered into the refrigerator at the array of Mexican food that she hadn't touched the evening before.

Greasy fajitas for breakfast? Why not? she decided with a shrug. Her hand was on the container of seasoned chicken strips and veggies when she spotted the orchid corsage half-hidden by a carton of milk. She forgot about fajitas for a moment as she lifted out the corsage. With dismay, she saw that the bloom was shriveled and brown. She touched a shrunken petal; it quivered like a leaf in a stiff breeze and fell off, drifting to the floor. The flower was obviously beyond preserving. Sighing, Kayla wrapped the corsage in a piece of old newspaper, as if she were preparing it for burial, and placed it in the trash bin she kept under the sink.

Over her breakfast of oven-warmed fajitas, Kayla made up her mind to go to the arena. Even if she couldn't put on her skates yet, what harm would it cause her to sit in the stands and watch the action on the ice? She hadn't a clue as to what she might do — or say — if she ran into Ryan, though whether he'd even show up at the rink was open to question. Last night, she'd convinced herself that if he wanted to believe she was involved with Hamil, it was for the best. But in the fresh light of morning, she wasn't so sure of her wisdom on the matter.

Two things were clear to her. She was helplessly in love with Ryan — as Meghan had so plainly pointed out to her. And she couldn't bear the thought of another man holding her. The memory of Ryan's kisses made her heart soar, her blood sing. The idea that she might never know his kiss, his tender embrace again sent her free-falling into a pit of dark despair.

With trembling hands, Kayla got her jacket from the bedroom closet. She walked back through the living room to the phone. *Better now than later,* she told herself as she lifted the receiver and dialed Hamil's number. She might be taking the coward's way out, praying that she would get the agent's answering machine. But how could she explain to him that her life had been thrown a steep curve, that she wasn't certain of much these days except for the war going on between her heart and mind?

"Hi, it's Kayla," she said, when Hamil's recorder came on. "I'm sorry, but the twenty-fourth and twenty-fifth won't work out for me. Maybe another time," she added, conscious there wouldn't be another time.

Kayla drove across town amid heavy morning traffic. There was a sprinkling of snow on the ground; it sparkled like sugar in the sunshine. The brightness hurt Kayla's eyes so that she wanted to squeeze them shut. Or was it the hot tears lurking behind her lids that made her squint?

By the time she pulled into the arena's parking lot her nerves were tingling and her hands were freezing, despite the warm air from the heater. At least her ankle felt a little less sore, and she was able to walk without too much of a noticeable limp. After her shower that morning, she'd exercised the ankle in the warm and cold baths, then wrapped it snugly in Ryan's socks and the elastic bandage. Maybe following Dr. Quintana's orders was paying off. *It has to,* she thought, *because I'm not missing this competition.*

A check of the parking lot showed no sign of Ryan's car. Shielding her face against the wind, Kayla headed for the arena, then changed her mind and veered toward the café. Most of the other skaters would be on the rink, so she should be able to sit in the restaurant in relative peace for a while.

As she'd hoped, the café was nearly deserted, and she didn't recognize any of the few diners. Still, she ducked her head as she sought out a booth in the back.

The waitress came, and Kayla placed her order of coffee with cream. Staring out the window, she tried to anticipate how she would handle facing Ryan in the morning when they met for the first time on the ice since before the party. She imagined an awkward scene, each of them avoiding the other's eyes while one or the other of them dredged up some innocuous comment about the weather or the roughness of the ice.

Her coffee arrived and she drank a couple of swallows, curving her fingers around the mug to ease the chill in them. Not just her fingers, but her whole body felt cold, so cold that she began to wonder if even the heat of the summer sun could warm her.

"Ah, I see our fair Kayla is on the mend."

Her head jerked up, and she had to stifle a cry as her eyes met Fletcher's. "What are you doing here?" she demanded without thinking.

His brows arched. "Oh, touchy, touchy this morning, aren't we? But that's to be expected after your accident."

She almost choked on her coffee.

A dry, throaty chuckle rose in Fletcher's throat. "You should know how difficult it is to keep such a thing under wraps, Kayla." He tossed a section of folded newspaper onto the table. "Especially when you're the lead story."

The headline splashed across the top of the page blared out at her. *Will Skater's Injury Doom Pair's Chances in Upcoming Competition?*

Kayla barely noticed Fletcher's retreat from the booth as she began to read the short, two-column article:

Kayla Quinn, of the number-one ranked pairs team, Quinn and Maxwell, sustained an injury to her ankle when she fell under unknown circumstances on the front steps of Timberfrost Lodge. The mishap occurred the evening of the dinner party held for local figure skaters and their coaches.

The article went on to question whether the "unfortunate accident" would force Quinn and Maxwell to withdraw from the Golden Skates. There was more than a hint of doubt as to the pair's chances of competing at Worlds. An unflattering file photo accompanied the article.

Kayla threw the paper aside and drank her coffee in unladylike gulps. Her cheeks flamed with anger. Her first impulse was to call the reporter and let him know that Kayla Quinn planned on being a fierce competitor for the title in the Golden Skates *and* Worlds, thank you. But her anger cooled slightly when she realized that she'd be setting herself up for a barrage of questions from the intrepid reporter — perhaps more than one of them to do with rumors of a romance between the duo of Quinn and Maxwell. How had the media latched onto the news about her accident to begin with?

Kayla knew the answer as soon as she glanced up and saw Fletcher standing at the register, paying his bill. His gaze was glued on her, and his smarmy smile telegraphed more loudly than words that he was the culprit who had snitched on her.

It made perfect sense. He hated Eve; he was itching to get even. And Ryan had fueled Fletcher's fires of revenge when he branded him the royal toad, shaming him in front of his adoring "fan club."

Kayla didn't move so much as a muscle until Fletcher was gone. Then she folded the paper so that the headline and article were hidden from view and tucked it under her arm. She held her head high despite the fact that the other diners were watching her exit and she imagined they were whispering "too bad, too bad," behind their hands.

She crossed the street and slipped through a rear door of the arena. Then she took the service elevator to the balcony where she would have an eagle's-eye view of the ice without the risk of being seen by anyone below.

Kayla sat through the morning in the hard balcony seat, observing the action on the ice. She secretly applauded Meghan's near-flawless rehearsal of her long program and caught herself holding her breath as Mitchell executed a fast series of spectacular triple axels. Mitchell was impressive on the ice; someday he could overtake Scott as men's champion — or at the least inherit Scott's title when he retired. She remembered Ryan's assertion that Mitchell had a crush on her, and she smiled to herself. So Ryan *had* been jealous.

At noontime, Kayla reached for the granola bars she always had stashed in her jacket. All the while she kept an eye out for her partner. He had yet to show up. For that matter, so had Christy.

Kayla's mind took a wild spin. Could it

be possible that the two of them . . . She didn't allow herself to finish the thought. Rising quickly from her seat, she left the balcony.

When the service elevator creaked to a stop on the first floor, Kayla cautiously peered up and down the hallway. The corridor was empty, and she stepped out, intent on slipping away undetected. The echo of footsteps prompted her to toss a glance over her shoulder. Too late she realized the footsteps were approaching from the opposite direction. Like an actor in a bad comedy, she walked right into Ryan's arms.

"Kayla?" He grasped her by the shoulders and stared down at her with a disapproving scowl. "What are you doing here?"

"I —"

"You're not supposed to be on the ice until tomorrow," he cut in.

She met his demanding gaze with one of her own. "As you can see, I'm not on the ice," she bristled. "I don't recall Dr. Quintana ordering me to stay away from the stands." A shiver shot through her at the feel of his hot breath on her face. Why did he have to look so maddeningly appealing in his red flannel shirt and faded denims? "I suppose you haven't seen this."

She thrust the newspaper under his nose and watched his expression change from impertinence to shock.

He let go of her and grabbed the paper in his hands. "How in the . . ."

She rubbed her arms where his fingers had held her tight. "Fletcher," she said, "who else? He approached me in the café and made a point of giving me the newspaper."

Ryan's eyes flashed coldly. "The weasel."

"Don't, Ryan." Her heart contracted as she reached out to touch his arm. This time he didn't withdraw from her. "We'll show Fletcher — everyone — that we can beat the odds and win."

He made no response, only looked at her with an expression that changed before her eyes from fury to despair. "I called Bill last night," he said. "Told him I'd be coming to New York right after Worlds. He gave me the names and numbers of a couple of agents. In case things don't work out between you and Brookings — or whoever." He pressed a piece of paper into her palm and folded her fingers over it.

Kayla stared at her closed hand. Her mind comprehended her partner's words, their logic, but her heart rebelled against them.

Ryan cupped her chin in his fingers, forcing her to look up. "Go home, Kayla. I'll see you tomorrow."

A feeling of hopelessness gripped her as she watched him walk off. When he disappeared from sight around a corner, she walked slowly to the exit and let herself out.

Sitting alone on a hard, wooden bench in the men's locker, Ryan mapped out a killer schedule for himself. Bumping into Kayla in the corridor had shaken him badly. Seeing that article about her in the daily rag, knowing that Fletcher must've been behind it had set his blood boiling. All his protective instincts had rallied to the fore. He'd almost lost control of himself again, come within a hair's breadth of telling Kayla that he loved her.

In truth, what he'd wanted — no, longed — to do was carry her off to a place, any place, where they wouldn't risk being discovered, and show her without words exactly how much he cherished her.

And that was the very reason why he had to devise a new game plan, one that would leave him exhausted at the end of each day. Too exhausted to think of her, to think of anything but sleep. If he stuck to his regimen, he might be able to cope, make it through the Golden Skates, Worlds even, and keep his sanity intact in the bargain.

The afternoon didn't get any easier for Ryan. As soon as he hit the ice, he was bombarded with inquiries about Kayla's state of health. Once the story broke, the rumors must have spread fast. But he did his best to assure the skaters and judges and members of the press who hung on his every word that Kayla was doing great and would be back on skates in the morning. All he could do after the crowd dissipated was hope he'd satisfied their curiosity.

When the club's practice ended that evening, he set his plan in motion. He spent the better part of the next three hours at a health club he hadn't frequented in a while. He got a massage, exercised his knee under the eye of a trainer, and sat in the sauna, coaxing his muscles to relax.

Later, back at his apartment, he wolfed down an apple and a peanut-butter sandwich. Then he fell into bed, ready to drop off to sleep.

That's where his plan to keep his mind off of Kayla hit the skids. He lay on his back, staring at a corner of the wall near his bed, where a little circle of moonlight played over the ragged edges of a cobweb.

He told himself he should be pleased that he'd made it plain to Kayla he was moving ahead with his intentions to join Bill after Worlds. That left her free and clear to pursue a career, hook up with a tour, date Brookings, hire him as her agent — if she was foolish enough to trust him.

Ryan's fist connected with his pillow, narrowly missing the headboard of the bed. He cursed his bad luck, his bum knee, his former weakness for Gillian, his father's cheating ways, his own pride — and any other person or idea that came into his head.

How could he even toy with the idea of a future with Kayla? Worse, how could they continue as they were, pretending to be just friends and holding each other like lovers?

But suppose he did lay his cards on the table, tell her he loved her and wanted her to stay in his life? What then? Offer her a proposal of marriage — and a job at Bill's rink? He couldn't imagine Kayla being content coaching on the sidelines when she belonged in the spotlight, deserved to be there. And he couldn't imagine going on without her.

Sometime before morning he must've

dozed off because the next thing he knew he heard the jangling of the alarm clock, telling him it was time to rise and shine.

Ryan arrived at the arena a hair before five-thirty, only to find that Kayla was already there, doing her warm-ups. He was glad to see that she seemed as determined as he was to keep their practices all business. In deference to her ankle and his knee, they concentrated on their footwork and their lifts and spins.

Still, it was with a silent sigh of relief that he parted from her at the end of a long afternoon practice session. Over dinner at the café, he told himself to hang tough. It was seven days and counting until the start of the competition.

Chapter Fourteen

"That was excellent, Shelly. A perfect Salchow." Kayla bent to put her arm around the young girl.

Shelly gazed up at her. "I'm going to do a perfect one at the Golden Skates, too."

"I'm sure you will. Why don't we try the whole routine? I'd like to see your sit spin."

Shelly started off, then darted back to Kayla. Without warning, she flung her arms around Kayla and hugged her.

Kayla gently set the girl away from herself. "What was that for?" she asked, smiling. Shelly was entirely too precious. No wonder Charlie and Joan were so proud of her.

"You looked kind of sad. My mom says my hugs are the best cure she knows of to make her feel better when she's had a bad day."

Kayla took the girl back in her embrace. "Your mom's right, Shelly. Your hug helped a lot." Watching Shelly skate off, she realized she hadn't been completely successful in hiding her melancholy from others.

After her encounter with Ryan in the hallway the day before, she'd come to the conclusion that whatever feelings they had for each other, he had made up his mind to put it all behind him. Hadn't he made that clear to her when he'd pointedly told her that he was moving to Winding River after Worlds and pressed the names and telephone numbers of the agents into her hand?

She wondered how he would rationalize away the sparks that flew between them whenever their eyes met, or the newly possessive way he held her during their routines. The passion they were known for in their performances was definitely back. But there was a difference now — an almost palpable need that manifested itself in his every touch, her every response. A need that he was obviously determined to ignore.

Shelly skated to the boards, and all at once Kayla realized she had been paying only token attention to the girl's routine. "That was very good," she commended a bit guiltily. Kayla sensed from the girl's expression that Shelly was anticipating some word of advice. "Remember, when you go into the sit spin, you need to keep your right leg extended." Kayla demonstrated the position and Shelly followed in imitation. Then with a pat on Shelly's arm, she dismissed the girl for the evening.

Close by, Ryan was busy instructing Petey. At the sound of his voice, Kayla glanced over at him. Ryan's eyes made contact with hers. They stared at each other over the frozen expanse of ice until Kayla was compelled to look away. When she sneaked another glance at him, she saw that he was turned the other way, and she skated off on legs that felt as if they belonged on a rubber chicken.

Later, outside the women's dressing room, Meghan caught up with her. "Are you in a hurry?"

Kayla offered her friend a tired smile. "I'm ready to go home and get some sleep."

"How's your ankle today?"

"It's stiff, a little sore. But I can't complain."

"Well, from all appearances I'd say that some very positive things have been going on between you and Ryan. You two looked as if you were about to melt the ice."

Kayla slumped against the wall. "No. The truth is that things couldn't be worse between us."

"I'm so sorry. Do you want to talk about it?"

"There's nothing to talk about. Ryan and I . . . We just got sidetracked for a few days, and now . . ."

Meghan looped her arm through Kayla's. "Sidetracked is one thing. Falling in love is another."

"It would never have worked out, Meghan."

"I detect a note of uncertainty."

Kayla stared at the ceiling, near tears. "Ryan's under the impression that I'm dating Hamil. I thought it would be easier for both of us if he believed I was seeing another man." She blinked back the wetness. "I even had the crazy notion that he's made up with Christy."

"Ryan definitely hasn't made up with Christy."

Kayla met her friend's eyes. Meghan was smiling. "How can you be sure?"

"Because Christy's left town."

"What?"

"Absolutely true. I learned from a very reliable source — Mitchell — that Christy withdrew from the competition yesterday and left unexciting little Colorado Springs lock, stock, and barrel. On Sully Vancoff's arm."

"She went with her agent to Hollywood?"

Meghan laughed. "More like her latest boyfriend — and her ticket to stardom. So she thinks."

Kayla had to admit that the idea of Christy flitting off to L.A. wasn't so far-fetched, after all. "At least we won't have to put up with her in the competition."

"You know, I'll kind of miss the challenge. Realizing that Christy was out to steal the title made me push myself harder. But . . ." Meghan patted Kayla's hand. "Getting back to more important matters. Like you and Ryan, for instance. Sometimes you have to let go of fear, Kayla, be willing to take a chance."

"You mean forget the career I've worked like a dog for my whole life, forfeit my dreams of turning pro."

"Not exactly. Think of it as trading one dream for another that will lead to even greater happiness and contentment."

Perhaps, thought Kayla, unable to bring herself to confess how tempting the idea sounded to her at the moment. Nor how frightened she still was that a wrong decision would lead not to happiness, but heartbreak.

"Can you in all honesty say that you want to tour as a singles skater?" Meghan began to steer her toward the exit that led to the parking lot. "Don't tell me. You have to search your heart and answer that question for yourself. Just remember, Kayla, what's most important is to be at peace with your decision."

Ryan woke on Wednesday morning to find a message from Eve on his answering machine. She instructed him not to pick her up at the airport on her arrival in the afternoon. Instead, she would come directly from the airport to the arena in the terminal's courtesy van. Her flight was due in at two-thirty and, with any luck, she should be at the rink by 4:00 p.m., she said, concluding her monologue with "Give my love to Kayla and don't take the afternoon off, waiting for me to waltz in."

Ryan smiled to himself as he switched off the machine and went to the chest of drawers to retrieve fresh socks and a T-shirt. Hearing his coach's voice made him realize how much he'd missed her.

It would be good to have her back. Maybe her presence would serve to ease some of the strain between Kayla and himself. Or, he thought, pulling a pair of navy wool socks from the top drawer, maybe it would complicate an already tense situation.

By the time Eve came streaking across the ice at five minutes to four, Ryan felt like a man walking a highwire. The only things he and Kayla had agreed on the whole day were that they should tell Eve about the ankle injury and clue her in on Marty's suggestion concerning their long program. He wasn't inclined to mention his gimpy knee, though Kayla had argued that he should. It wasn't the first time he'd had to pamper it, and with Worlds looming just around the corner, it wouldn't be the last.

After the usual greetings and hugs, Kayla broke the news to Eve about her sprain. An expression of mild shock registered on the coach's face. Otherwise, she appeared unruffled about the whole affair. But then Eve was generally adept at covering up her emotions.

But as the coach leveled her green eyes at his partner, then at him, Ryan grew antsy. Eve was cunning and watchful — like the tigress he sometimes compared her to — and he doubted either he or Kayla were accomplished enough actors to convince her that everything was fine and dandy with the troops.

"Well," the coach said at last, "I like Marty's suggestion. Let's see how it works." She waved a hand in the air.

When Eve cleared her throat, Ryan took it as a signal to get moving. He flashed a phony grin at the coach, and Kayla flashed a fake smile at him. "What are we waiting for?" he said, grabbing his partner's hand and leading the way to the center of the ice.

By the end of the week, Ryan felt as if he'd hiked to the 14,400-foot summit of Pikes Peak and back — barefoot and driven by a madman with a whip. There was no madman, just Eve, who had increased the length of his and Kayla's practices to the point where he didn't need a session at the health club to get him in the mood for sleep at night.

But he'd been pushing, too, determined to give the Golden Skates his very best shot. It was for Kayla's sake, he told himself; everything was for her sake now.

As he walked through the corridor past the coaches' offices late Friday afternoon, his mind was more occupied with the club's practice that evening than with the coming competition. He'd picked up the kids' costumes during his lunch break, and the club would be having a full dress rehearsal in a couple of hours. Everyone but he and Kayla would be in costume. With a flurry of apologies, Estelle had explained to him that she'd have to make a few final adjustments in the pair's outfits. That was fine by him; he wasn't particularly anxious to suit up in the tux anyway.

"Ryan, is that you?"

The familiar sound of his coach's voice brought him up short. He stuck his head around the open door of her office.

"I knew those were your footsteps." The coach regarded him from where she sat behind her desk. "Come in and sit down for a minute, I have something for you." She held a piece of paper aloft.

Not another "love triangle," he fervently hoped as he took the chair across from Eve. No doubt she'd heard the news about Christy leaving for Tinseltown with Vancoff. He was prepared if she brought up the subject, ready to let her know that he'd broken off with Christy before she'd decided to pack things in at the rink. What he was not about to tell the coach was that his love for Kayla was eating him up inside.

"I want you to know that I'm very pleased with your practices. The judges are taking notice, too." Eve's eyes sparkled. "Maybe I should go away more often."

Ryan cast the coach a wary smile. Her commendation was nice to hear, especially since Lamore and Stratton and the Kapinskys had arrived and were now sharing the ice with himself and Kayla. But he knew Eve well enough to realize that she was leading up to something more.

"I just received this fax from Bill." The coach gave him the piece of paper she had in her hands. "He told me about it over the phone. He was certain you'd be interested in the report because it might help you extend the length of your skating career."

What now? he thought as he looked at the sheet. The title "New Laser Technique Revolutionizes Surgery for Athletic Injuries" caught his eye.

"The article was written by the orthopedic surgeon who pioneered the procedure," Eve explained. "The wording is a bit technical, I'm afraid, but Bill was emphatic when he said he thought you should give it a try. Conveniently, the surgeon in question practices at Swedish Medical in Denver. If you're interested, I'd encourage you to make an appointment with him as soon as the competition is over."

"So Bill figures this surgery could help my knee?"

"Yes, and I agree with him."

Ryan tried to absorb the gist of the medical jargon on the page. "Just the other evening I promised Bill I'd start working for him right after Worlds. Everything's pretty well set for me," he added, all the while wondering, *Is it possible this laser thing could do the trick on my knee? But what about the cost?*

As if she'd anticipated the question, Eve offered, "Your insurance should cover the expense, if that's a concern, Ryan. And don't worry. Bill wants you to coach for him. But he also suspects you may not be ready to turn in your skates — or end your partnership with Kayla."

Ryan's throat suddenly felt as dry as the plains east of Colorado Springs. "I never told Bill that."

"You didn't need to," the coach returned with a smile. "He said the tone of your voice gave you away. I think you know that Bill's right. Now" — Eve reached for a pile of notes that were held together with a huge clip — "please excuse me. I have a ton of calls to make."

Ryan rose numbly from his chair. He

started to go, then paused, remembering his manners. "Thanks, Eve," he said. "I'll at least look the article over."

"You're welcome," he heard her say as he walked out the door.

Late Sunday afternoon Kayla stood with Ryan on the ice, waiting for their coach to open the slip of paper she held in her hand.

Finally, Eve ended the suspense. "The luck of the draw," she quipped, passing the slip to Kayla.

Releasing a breath, Kayla peeked at the number written on the paper. *Four.* She and Ryan would skate their short program fourth in a field of eight pairs. She hated the placement almost as much as she did when they drew the first or second slot. Beside her, Ryan gave a grunt of disapproval.

"Look at it this way," Eve said, draping an arm around each of them. "It has to get better with the long program."

Kayla couldn't think that far ahead. She could barely think at all. Or eat. Or sleep. The fact was she'd been living and skating on sheer strength of will and little else the past week.

At least there was no rehearsal scheduled

for the club that day, so when Eve dismissed her students, Kayla beat a hasty retreat with Ryan for the nearest exit.

"Ah, Kayla." Fletcher stepped in front of her. "Joyous day." His gaze narrowed in on Ryan. "Someone very special is here to see you, fair lady."

Fletcher's expression — like the cat that had just lapped up the cream — put Kayla on red alert as she followed his grand gesture.

There, striding toward her with a broad smile on his face and an armful of red roses, was Hamil Brookings.

Chapter Fifteen

"Hamil . . ." Kayla stared at the agent, stunned. His pinstriped suit and sleek dark hair, with a sprinkling of silver at the temples, lent an urbane appearance to his polished good looks. "What are you doing here?"

He chuckled; his hazel eyes danced with light.

"Surprising you, it would seem. I realize this is only the twenty-second, but I wrapped up a couple of interviews in Vegas a day early, and I have to confess I was far more anxious to see you than try my luck at blackjack."

Kayla took an involuntary step backward as he closed the space between them and pressed the roses into her hands. "But, didn't you . . ." she began, then stopped. It dawned on her that if he'd been in Las Vegas, he wouldn't have gotten her message. Suddenly she remembered Ryan.

He'd been right behind her. She saw no sign of him either on the ice or in the corridor, and a sinking sense of despair settled in her stomach.

"Shall we go, Kayla? I'll wait for you outside the dressing rooms."

Before she could respond, Hamil's arm slipped firmly around her waist.

He didn't seem to notice her silence as he went on, "I've made reservations for dinner for two at Sunstone. And that's only for starters," he whispered, his breath blowing hotly in her ear.

"To me," Scott declared, "this sounds like an answer to a prayer." He passed back to Ryan the article on the new laser knee surgery.

Ryan stuffed the article into his pocket. "Yeah, maybe," he said.

"Don't bowl me over with your optimism," Scott joked.

Ryan didn't laugh. His mind was too busy trying to absorb the fact that Brookings was in Colorado Springs.

"What did Kayla have to say about it?"

"Huh? Oh, you mean the knee surgery. I haven't discussed it with her."

"You haven't told her about something that could change the course of the future for the two of you?"

Ryan scanned the locker room before replying. "An operation isn't going to change our future," he said gruffly. "Not when Brookings is part of hers."

"Brookings? I think you're imagining things, bud."

"Then I must be hallucinating, too, because fifteen minutes ago I saw him waiting for Kayla in the hall."

"You're kidding — no, you're not. Hey, maybe the guy's here strictly on business."

Ryan barked out a laugh. "With an armload of red roses?"

"Then all I have to say is that's even more reason for you to get on the stick and tell her that you're in love with her." Scott paused. "You know, I think the problem here is that you're running scared — and too proud to admit it."

"Scared? I'm only considering what's best for Kayla, maybe for myself as well. There's no way of knowing at this point whether the surgery will do the job on my knee or not. If it doesn't . . ." He looked at the floor. There was a wad of purple chewing gum stuck on the wooden boards near his right toe. If he moved his foot an inch, the gum would be decorating his shoe. *Courtesy of one of Fletch's googly-eyed fans, no doubt,* he thought with disgust.

"No," Scott was saying. "The trouble isn't whether or not your knee's going to get fixed up. The problem is that you're still licking your wounds from when you and Gillian called it quits and she hooked up with Tyler. If my memory serves me right, you were ready to give up the sport yourself."

Chad Tyler. The name struck a hateful chord in Ryan. *The ultimate closet junkie. And the beginning of the end for Gillian's shot at a skating career.* "Maybe I should've given it up," he said with rancor.

Scott shook his head. "It was a good thing that Bill talked sense into that obstinate brain of yours. But we've hashed that all out before, Ryan. There's no crime in loving someone. Just because Gillian didn't return your feelings doesn't mean those feelings were wrong. No one knew that Tyler was doing drugs — not even his coach. He had everyone fooled for a while. Including Gillian."

Ryan's jaw tightened. "Don't you see? I drove her to Tyler. Gillian and I would still be a team today, winning championships, if

I'd kept my heart — and my hands — under control."

"Are you saying you regret pairing up with Kayla?"

The question cut him to the quick. How could he regret the five great years they'd had together on the ice? "Of course not. It's just . . ." Ryan raked a hand through his hair. "I felt protective of Gillian, that she was vulnerable." *The same way I feel toward Kayla. Only more so with Kayla,* he realized. "I can't seem to shake the idea that I let her down in the worst kind of way."

"Gillian also knew how to play on your emotions," Scott said with unusual sharpness. "Listen to me, bud," he went on in a gentler tone. "If Kayla loves you — and I think deep inside yourself you know the answer to that — then you're what she needs, not some life alone on the road."

"Kayla *had* been showing a few signs that she cared for me," Ryan conceded.

"More than a few, I'll bet. You'd better 'fess up soon to her. Let her decide. I think you're going to be real happy with the outcome." Scott reached over to clasp hold of Ryan's hand as they rose from the bench.

Ryan returned the handshake, but he couldn't bring himself to promise Scott that he would follow through on his advice.

Kayla's eyes were focused on the contract Hamil had pushed in front of her, but her mind couldn't seem to process the meaning of the numbers printed on the page.

"I'm certain I can persuade Vogel to make even more concessions," Hamil said. He tossed her a charming grin as he leaned back in his chair and folded his arms over his chest.

The agent had treated her to lobster and Grand Marnier soufflé. He'd regaled her with stories and witty asides about the famous and not-so-famous of Hollywood moviedom. He'd played the part of the perfect gentleman, treating her with thoughtful respect throughout the evening. Most significantly, he'd kept his hands to himself, though his eyes had sent more than one smoldering signal that his interest in her was far from purely professional.

She'd dutifully eaten the lobster and soufflé. She'd smiled and laughed at his tales. She'd murmured her appreciation for the little courtesies he'd shown her. And all the while her eyes had been sending him signals that her interest in him was strictly professional — at best.

Kayla raised her head. From the expression on Hamil's face, it was obvious that her silent messages hadn't gotten through. She cleared her throat.

"I'll need some time to consider this," she said. "I didn't expect to be presented with a proposal for a contract this evening."

Hamil lifted his wine glass and smiled at her over the rim. "Take the time you need, but I feel confident that you won't find a sweeter deal with any other company. Vogel's Ice Castles Tour is top-drawer, Kayla." His eyes narrowed the slightest degree. "You must be seriously considering your future, since you've openly declared your intention to turn pro after Worlds in Vienna."

At the mention of Vienna, images of a certain snow-frosted Tyrolean-style inn popped into Kayla's head. On her one previous visit to Austria's enchanting capital, she had viewed the cozy hotel from the blanketed warmth of a horse-drawn carriage that she, Ryan, and Eve had secured for a tour of the city. She had been utterly captivated by the old inn's gingerbread house–type charm.

The inn would be the perfect place for a honeymoon, she thought. The feel of Hamil's cool fingers covering hers snapped her back to reality.

"Yes," she said quickly, "my intention is to tour."

"And I'd say we've talked enough business for now," Hamil announced. His gaze was fixed on her lips, and his mouth twitched up at the corners. "Why don't we retire to the piano bar downstairs," he suggested in an intimate tone.

"I'm sorry." Kayla snatched her hand away from his on the pretext of searching for a tissue in her purse. "I have a competition coming up, and . . . I really need to go home and nurse this throbbing ankle," she added, stretching the truth. She dabbed at her nose with the tissue.

"By all means." Hamil motioned for the waiter. After the bill had been paid, he came around to Kayla's chair. "Do you know that your beauty intoxicates me?" he whispered, pressing his palm against the small of her back as she rose from the chair.

Kayla swallowed back a wave of dismay. There was only one man that she wanted to intoxicate, one man whose touch she craved. But hadn't Ryan himself as good as given her a shove in the agent's direction by urging her to obtain representation as soon as possible? With a tight smile frozen on her lips, she moved past Hamil and scooted just out of his reach.

Chapter Sixteen

The beginning day of the Golden Skates dawned cheerless and blustery. As Kayla made her way through the empty concourses of the arena to the curving stairwell that led up to the balcony, she tried very hard to keep her mood from matching the weather. In the past, regardless of the weather outside or even her own state of health, she'd been able to psyche herself up for a competition, to summon the positive thoughts and visual images that helped her rise to her best level of performance on the ice. But that was when she'd been smart enough to focus all of her energies on her career, before she'd let her heart win the war over her mind and fallen in love with her partner.

The days leading up to the start of the competition had passed like a sequence of bad dreams for Kayla. Marathon practices had left her physically exhausted at the end of each evening. But spending every moment of those hours on the ice with Ryan had sent her emotions careening nearly out of control. And Hamil Brookings's ill-timed appearance in Colorado Springs had only complicated an already impossible situation. Hamil was gone now, and she had let him know when he'd tried to kiss her at her front door the evening he'd taken her to dinner that there was no hope of a romantic relationship between them. To his credit, he'd told her that his contract proposal was still firm. So she'd kept the piece of paper, half tempted to sign and return it to Hamil posthaste, yet holding back, balking at the simple task of picking up a pen and putting her name on the appropriate line.

Gingerly mounting the stairs, Kayla tested her ankle for weakness. It felt good, almost normal. Thanks to Ryan, she knew. Wasn't that when she'd begun to acknowledge the depth of her feelings for him — the night she'd sprained her ankle and he'd shown such tender concern for her?

She took the steps faster, as if by picking up her pace she could distance herself from her love for Ryan. At the top of the stairs, she paused for breath. Then she opened the door with the glowing red

EXIT sign and was enfolded by the darkness of the upper balcony. Below, the rink was aglow with lights, a shimmering perfect pearl of ice. Kayla drank in its calming beauty. She listened appreciatively to the sound of utter silence that enveloped the arena, wishing she could absorb into her blood and bones the peaceful solitude of her surroundings. If she tried hard enough, she could almost make herself believe that the perfect pearl would never again be blemished by the clashing blades of hundreds of pairs of skates, that the quiet of that winter morning would never again be broken by the shouts and wild applause of thousands of enthusiastic fans.

Surveying tier after tier of empty seats, she set her gaze on the third row just behind the judges' booth, first and second seats. Closing her eyes, she saw in her mind the dented brass tags screwed to the scarred wooden arms of the chairs, identifying them as seats number 350 and 351. The chairs were the ones Cleo and Sharon traditionally occupied during the Golden Skates. Now strangers would be sitting in their places, and Kayla would have to look elsewhere for the inspiration she always drew from knowing her folks were in the stands, cheering her on.

But isn't that the answer? she asked herself. This was the last year she and Ryan would ever compete in the Golden Skates. This was the only year that Cleo and Sharon couldn't be there for them. Her natural parents had never seen her compete in the Golden Skates. They'd never seen her win a championship. Both sets of parents had enriched her life with abundant love and an unerring belief in her ability to do whatever she set out to accomplish. She made a vow in her heart that she wouldn't let them down now.

"Three-tenths of a point," Ryan said glumly.

Kayla stole a glance at her partner. They were sitting in the area known as "Kiss and Cry," where skaters and their coaches awaited the judges' decision in a competition. A look of disappointment spread over Ryan's face like dark clouds across the sky before a storm.

Kayla fought back a wave of despair. Three-tenths of a point separated Quinn and Maxwell from Lamore and Stratton, the current leaders after the short program in the Golden Skates. The Kapinskys and Chelsea and Justin had yet to skate, which opened up the possibility that she and

Ryan could drop to fourth place going into the long program phase of the competition.

Though the short program had never been their strong suit, Kayla suspected her partner was laying the blame on himself for their poor showing that evening. He'd stumbled on their side-by-side Salchows.

"You'll make it up in the long program," Eve consoled from where she sat on the other side of Ryan.

"Sure we will," he said.

Kayla felt his fingers entwine with hers. It was the first time he'd initiated any gesture toward her remotely resembling affection since Hamil's visit. There hadn't been so much as a mention of the agent's name by either of them, and off the ice, there'd been a woeful lack of communication between them. To make matters worse, Eve had been humoring them along to the point that Kayla felt her nerves would snap and she would say something to the coach that she would later live to regret.

Without warning, Ryan pulled his hand away from hers and got up from his chair. The roar of applause filled Kayla's ears. She fixed a smile on her face and raised her hand in a wave to the sympathetic crowd before following her partner and Eve to the exit.

To Kayla's chagrin, the press was waiting for them in the corridor. Since her ankle injury, she had dodged the media as much as possible, even though recent reports on Quinn and Maxwell had taken a more favorable turn. As flashbulbs popped and microphones were thrust in front of her, she had a sudden violent urge to make a dash for the dressing rooms. But then Ryan stepped in and handled the reporters' questions, fielding their inquiries into what went wrong for the pair on the ice that afternoon.

Just when Kayla thought the press was finished with them for the day, a reporter from *The Beacon*, a regional weekly newspaper, shouted, "Kayla, can you confirm the rumor that you're on the verge of signing a lucrative contract with the Brookings Agency for a berth on the Ice Castles Tour?"

Her heart gave a hard slam. Had Hamil leaked the news during his visit? Or had Fletcher played the tattletale again?

"I . . ." She moistened her lips with her tongue. "I'm not prepared to comment on that at the present." She glanced at Ryan. His dark eyes impaled hers for an instant.

"Thank you," he told the press with all

the grim formality of an undertaker over-seeing a funeral. "Now if you'll excuse us, Kayla and I have to be somewhere in an hour."

His hand at her elbow, he steered her along the empty concourse to the women's dressing rooms, where he addressed her with only a curt, "See you tomorrow."

There wasn't a car or a human being in sight as Ryan brought his BMW to a crunching halt in the gravel parking lot near Prospect Lake.

No wonder, he thought, emerging from the car. With the wind assaulting his face like sharp, icy needles and the sun already sinking behind the Peak against a sickly purple sky, he must be crazy to be out for a hike around the lake.

Maybe I have finally gone over the edge. When he'd left Kayla at the arena after his sloppy performance in the short program, he'd felt like running to the park and back about a dozen times just to cool his frustration.

Heck, he was lucky he could still walk — or that he could lace up his skates and make it through the short program at all. Despite the pampering he'd lavished on his knee, the discomfort had grown worse. So had the gnawing pain in the vicinity of his heart.

Since his conversation with Scott, he'd done some heavy-duty thinking. Should he plunge ahead and ask Kayla to marry him? The idea that he might be setting himself up for a turn down from her gave him cold sweats.

But what could be worse than not taking the chance she might answer in the affirmative to his proposal? *On the other hand,* the voice of doubt inside his head whispered, *if Scott is wrong, and she is deeply involved with Brookings, or if she has signed a contract . . .* He imagined her exquisitely beautiful face pulled into a pained expression of regret when she told him that she couldn't marry him because she was in love with someone else.

The hurt of knowing he couldn't promise her the bright, exciting future that a man of Brookings's stature could offer her cut through him as sharply as the bitter gale howling off the Peak.

Despite his throbbing knee, he increased his pace until he came to the bench that he and Kayla had shared just days before. That afternoon seemed like a lifetime ago to Ryan. He sat down and stared at the lake. Everything was gray and frigid in the gathering darkness. Even the birds and squirrels that usually skittered around the benches looking for a handout had burrowed in for the night. *I should burrow in, too,* he thought. *Head for home.*

Home. The word echoed in his head, and he realized that no place — not even Winding River — would ever really be home to him unless he had Kayla by his side. That's how it had been for a very long time, whether he wanted to acknowledge the fact or not.

On Friday, just before noon, a harried-looking courier delivered Kayla's and Ryan's costumes, along with a written note of apology from Estelle for the delay. At five o'clock, they learned that they'd hit the "luck of the draw." They would skate last among the field of eight pairs in the long program the next evening. Lamore and Stratton had drawn the next to the last slot, while the Kapinskys, who were a scant one-tenth of a point behind Quinn and Maxwell after the short program, would skate first.

Late Saturday afternoon, Kayla sat alone in front of the mirror in the women's dressing room of the arena, applying her makeup. Her costume hung on a rack nearby, and the box containing her head-band lay on a shelf. When she finished with her makeup, she took down the box and lifted out the headband.

The satin roses gleamed in the lights from the mirror. Unlike the orchid cor-sage, these blooms would never wither and die. Stroking the soft feathers that ac-cented the headband, Kayla wondered if she would keep the gift in remembrance of the day Ryan had given it to her. Or would it only serve as too painful a reminder of happier times?

Tears blurred her vision as she put the headband away. She thought of the sweater she'd knitted for Ryan. The project had given her something to do to occupy her restless hands each night. But the busy sound of the needles had made her think of the ticking of a clock — one that was sounding out the lonely minutes, hours, days of her future.

Kayla wiped a tear from her cheek and left the dressing room. She couldn't allow herself to cave in to tears now. As she walked the length of the concourse toward the rink, she conjured in her mind images of skating a flawless long program. At the entrance to the rink, she positioned herself near an exit sign so that she could watch

Meghan, who would be defending her title in a matter of minutes.

Gazing up at the rows of seats, Kayla located Charlie and Joan and several other sets of parents of the kids in the Crystal Palace Club. She waved to the families. A warm feeling wrapped around her when Shelly jumped up from her chair and pointed animatedly toward the ice.

I'll miss you, thought Kayla. She would miss all the kids in the club.

"Who are you so excited to see?"

Kayla froze at the sound of the familiar masculine voice. "Ryan . . . you're here."

"Did you think I'd miss Meghan's program?"

"No." Kayla devoured the sight of his face, his body that was suddenly so close to hers. He wore his navy warm-up suit; it was open at the neck, exposing a shock of curly dark chest hair. The words she meant to say wouldn't come as her eyes connected with Ryan's.

The boom of the announcer's voice over the P.A. broke the spell. Kayla tore her gaze from her partner and saw with mixed emotions that Scott was on his way to join them.

Though Scott looked relaxed, Kayla suspected that he just kept his anxiety well hidden behind a cheerful facade. He was bound to be nervous not only for Meghan but for himself, too. Fletcher had made a surprisingly strong showing in the short program, forging ahead of Scott by two-tenths of a point in the standings.

"Here comes Meggy now," Scott said with pride.

At the same instant Kayla turned her attention to the rink, Ryan's hands lightly grasped hold of her shoulders. While her eyes followed Meghan's performance, the rest of her basked in her partner's presence, and she could only think of how wonderful and right it felt to have him touching her at that moment.

On the ice, Meghan was skating flaw-lessly, executing her jumps and spins with precision and grace. By the time she went into her final moves, a triple-Salchow/double axel combination, the audience was on its feet, clapping and whistling.

Kayla impulsively threw her arms around Ryan's neck. "Meghan won! I'm sure of it."

"Me, too," he said. But already he was backing away from her. "I'll see you in a couple of hours," he told her, dropping his hands and his gaze.

She was stunned. "Where are you going?"

He didn't answer as he turned and melted into the crowd milling through the corridor. Without thinking twice, Kayla started after him, mumbling an excuse to Scott in passing.

A sickening, panicky feeling seized Kayla as she lost sight of her partner in the concourse. At last she spotted him heading for the men's locker room. Her pulse began to hammer in her ears when she saw how heavily he was favoring his bad leg.

"Ryan, wait!" she yelled out to him.

He stopped just short of the locker room door.

"Ryan, are you . . ."

"I'm all right."

They looked at each other, and gradually his face softened. He cupped her chin in his hand. "I'll *be okay,*" he said. His eyes riveted on hers for another heartbeat, then he ducked into the locker room.

"Ah, is there no end to lovers' quarrels?"

Kayla pivoted just in time to see Fletcher's lanky form bearing down on her. She held her tongue and resisted the urge to answer his stinging barb with one of her own. But the mocking sound of his laughter haunted her retreat, and her cheeks flamed with embarrassment as she brushed past the skaters and coaches who had witnessed the whole scene.

Two hours later, Kayla stood at her post by the exit where she had watched Meghan skate. Her gaze was fastened on the couple who had just taken center stage on the ice. Lamore and Stratton, dressed in dazzling red and black costumes, were ready to begin their long program, and Kayla felt compelled to watch. She had to know what odds she and Ryan were facing when it came their turn to skate.

Her stomach began to churn the second the pair's music came on. The melody was from the opera *Carmen*, a fitting choice for the skaters who were famous for their dramatic performances.

Lamore and Stratton opened with a breathtaking series of jumps and lifts, and Kayla's stomach tightened into a knot. The crowd's applause rang in her ears like the sound of doom as the couple went on to nail a triple Salchow and execute another series of lifts. The pair's footwork, a study in stunning synchronization, left Kayla feeling weak and envious. The possibility that she and Ryan could come from behind to capture the title seemed as unlikely to her as the idea that somehow she would find a way to convince Ryan that she loved him.

By the time the music came to a stirring conclusion, and Lamore and Stratton got ready to take their bows, Kayla wasn't sure she could stand the agony of waiting for the judges' scores to be posted. She feared they would all be perfect 6.0s.

Just then a warm, masculine hand engaged hers and drew her away. "Oh!" She gasped as Ryan coaxed her to come with him. He pulled her through a door that happened to be open, and she realized they were in Eve's office.

"Kayla . . ."

"Your knee . . ."

"Is wrapped up like a mummy." The next instant he swept her into a powerful embrace. "Nothing's going to stop us," he said against her hair. "Not my knee or your ankle. We'll win this one."

The affirmation struck a chord in Kayla; it was proof of his belief in himself, in her. Then their names sounded over the public address, and they stepped apart. It was time to show the world that the team of Quinn and Maxwell wasn't finished yet.

They were poised to go on the ice when Eve came up behind them. "Let your hearts lead you," she told them.

Kayla glanced at Ryan. He nodded. She held tightly to his hand as they skated to the middle of the ice and assumed their opening position facing the judges.

The applause from the audience died away, and there was an interminable pause before the music came on. Heat from the spotlights baked Kayla's face. The chill from the ice pricked at her legs. Every insecurity, every fear she'd ever known pressed in on her, and she said a silent prayer.

Then the first sweet notes of the saxophone solo came over the P.A. and Kayla felt Ryan's hand at her waist. They began to move across the ice, almost tentatively at first, then with more assurance as they followed an invisible path they had taken a thousand times before. Ryan lifted her into position for the double axel, then tossed her in the air. She felt as if she had wings as she spun in space and nailed a perfect landing on the ice.

Over the music she heard the acknowledging cheers of the crowd. She smiled into Ryan's eyes; he smiled into hers. The blood pounded in her head as they gathered speed and launched into their triple toe loops. Another roar of approval rocked the arena. The sympathy of the crowd was theirs once more, and Kayla sensed their momentum was building with every indelible mark their skates left on the ice.

The world was reduced to the two of them and the music and the crowd. On they glided through their side-by-side splits, their triple Lutzs and Salchows. The audience clapped in time to the music as they moved into the footwork portion of their program. On their hand-to-hand lift, Ryan gazed tenderly into her face, nestling her body close to his, making love to her with his eyes. A hush fell over the stands when the pair executed their death spiral.

Kayla throbbed with exhaustion as they neared the end of their program. Muscle memory kicked in, determination gave her the push she needed to complete her final jumps without an error. She and Ryan went into position for their last move, the sit spin. The audience was on its feet by the time Kayla came to a stop in Ryan's arms.

Her partner's features were drawn into an expression of triumph as he placed a kiss on her brow. Tears filled her eyes, and she said another prayer, one of gratitude. Despite everything — her ankle, his knee, their unresolved feelings for each other — they had beaten the odds and skated a program they could be proud of. She and Ryan took their bows as bouquets of flowers and stuffed animals rained onto the ice.

Back in Kiss and Cry, Eve greeted them with a hearty embrace. "Magnificent!" she enthused.

"Hopefully, it was enough," Ryan gasped out between labored breaths. He draped his arm around Kayla's shoulder while they awaited the judges' verdict.

Several long minutes passed until the announcer's voice crackled over the P.A. "Scores for technical merit for Quinn and Maxwell. 5.9, 5.9, 6.0." The crowd erupted into a frenzy of shouts and applause at the perfect score. When the din died down, the announcer went on, "6.0, 6.0, 6.0, 5.8." A collective groan filled the rink.

"Now the marks for artistic merit," the announcer continued. "6.0." The crowd went into hysterics again. "6.0, 5.9, 6.0, 6.0, 5.8."

"That's enough," Eve declared. "You did it."

"What did I tell you?" Ryan whispered the words in Kayla's ear as they skated back onto the ice to thank the crowd and the judges.

Kayla was relieved and happy. But the usual sense of giddy elation she knew on winning a championship was missing, and all she could think about was that soon she and Ryan would no longer be standing arm-in-arm on the ice, smiling and throwing kisses to an adoring crowd.

Meghan and Scott were there to greet them when they came off the ice. Meghan pressed a huge bouquet of mixed flowers into Ryan's arms and handed Kayla a folded white card.

Kayla stared at the flowers, then the card.

"Open it and you'll see," Meghan said.

Kayla read the message aloud. " 'Congratulations! We knew you could do it! All our love to you both, Cleo and Sharon.' " She looked at Ryan.

"Seems to me that your folks never doubted us," he said, placing the flowers in her arms.

"No," she agreed, remembering her vow to do her very best in the Golden Skates in honor of both her foster and her natural parents. She entrusted the bouquet to Eve so that she and Ryan could help the club members prepare for their number. Scott had yet to skate. The men's competition was slated last.

"Beat the skates off old Fletch," Ryan told his friend.

"Yes. Best of luck," Kayla added, hugging Scott.

"I'll keep you posted on the scores," Meghan promised.

A measure of confusion reigned in the women's dressing room when Kayla arrived. Club members and mothers in attendance clustered around her, buzzing with excitement. Estelle was there too, looking slightly frazzled as she took a couple of last-minute tucks in Gina's dress. Despite a mouthful of pins, she showered a broad smile on Kayla.

Within an hour Kayla, along with Estelle and the club-members' mothers, had managed to pull off a small miracle, getting the girls properly costumed and herded into the corridor where Ryan and the boys were already waiting. Gina burst into giggles, and Nathan stuck out his tongue at her. Shelly plucked at her headband and pulled loose a rose which Estelle scurried to reattach. Petey thrust his hands in his tux pockets and rocked on his heels until his shirttail came loose from his pants.

Kayla tried to catch Ryan's eye, but failed. All at once she wished the evening was over — the awards ceremony to come, the grand finale, the inevitable signing of autographs. Her body ached with the need to be alone with Ryan. But would she find the courage to tell him what was in her heart?

"It's over! Scott won! And Mitchell came in second."

Kayla spun around as Meghan came charging up to her. "Fletcher fell on both his triple Axels," Meghan announced with a grin.

"Way to go." Ryan kissed her on the cheek.

"Yeah," Petey said, raising his small hands in a victory sign.

Kayla couldn't help thinking that at last Fletcher had gotten his just deserts.

"Now, clubmembers." Ryan clapped his hands together. "It's almost show time."

Eve kept the kids corralled by the boards while the brief awards ceremony took place. On the podium, Kayla and Ryan accepted their medals, silver disks engraved with gold skates. Justin and Chelsea stood beside them, accepting their third-place medals in turn. The young pair had beaten the Kapinskys by a tenth of a point to win the bronze.

"And now, ladies and gentlemen, we have a special treat," the announcer said.

"The recently formed Crystal Palace Skating Club will bring the evening to an exciting conclusion."

"Okay, gang," Ryan said, "let's wow 'em."

The kids zipped onto the ice as their names were called. Whistles and applause went up from the stands when Kayla and Ryan skated out to join the clubmembers.

One by one the kids had their moment to shine. Shelly's hair glistened; her dress and headband made her look like a delicate buttercup under the lights. She executed her routine without a mistake, landing her Salchow to loud cheers. Gina, Nathan, Micah, Jennifer, and Drew followed in quick succession, skating their hearts out for the crowd.

Petey performed last, and Kayla knew the comfort of Ryan's hand enfolding hers as the boy took the spotlight. He started off in excellent form, grinning from ear to ear as he charged down the ice in preparation for his jump. But something must have happened on the way. Petey began to stumble. At the last second he caught himself and went on with aplomb to land a textbook-perfect toe loop. "Ohs" and "ahs" filled the air when he finished his routine.

The club fell into formation for the conga line and the audience rose, clapping in rhythm to the catchy Latin tune. The number came to a rousing conclusion to the accompaniment of shouts of "bravo!" and sustained applause.

Tears sprung in Kayla's eyes. Taking her bow with Ryan and the club, she realized she'd seen many dreams come true that night. All except the one she longed for most.

Charlie and Joan were waiting for Kayla near the boards. "Congratulations, Sunshine." Charlie gave her hand a hearty shake. "And the kids . . ." His face was radiant with pride. "The club put on a wonderful show."

Kayla hugged Joan and spoke with the couple for a few minutes. As she turned to go, a face in the crowd caught her eye. Glancing up, she recognized the man named Edward, who had stopped her outside the Pizza Connection with his wife that cold night. With him stood a heavyset girl, her blond hair pulled back in a thick braid. His daughter, Celia, no doubt. The girl waved in Kayla's direction, and Kayla was glad she'd remembered to send Celia a photo.

Soon, Kayla was beseiged by other fans,

and she graciously signed the pictures and programs that were pushed her way. Usually Ryan joined her, but not this time. After the crowd thinned out, she looked around for him. The rink was empty; it seemed that Ryan was gone.

Six months ago, winning a championship would have been just cause for a victory party. They would have celebrated with dinner at a nice restaurant — or, at the very least, with gourmet hamburgers and their favorite, hot fudge sundaes. But tonight —

The lights on the rink dimmed. The tiers of seats were empty as far as Kayla's eyes could see.

I should go, too, she thought, *home to my apartment and my fish.* A feeling of loneliness darkened her heart like the fringes of shadow that eclipsed the pearly oval of ice.

It's over, she told herself. *Ryan and I will never skate here together again in front of an audience. We'll never have the opportunity to defend our title in the Golden Skates. Doesn't that mean anything to him?*

Hot tears splashed down her cheeks. The quiet of the arena settled over her like a shroud. Still she stood at the edge of the ice, dressed in her costume and skates, unable to bring herself to walk away.

From a distance it seemed she heard music playing, an oddly familiar tune that softly shattered the silence. Puzzled, she looked around to see where it was coming from. Then a warm, strong hand came to rest on her shoulder, and she let out a little cry. "Ryan . . ."

He turned her toward him. His eyes met hers. "We never got to finish our dance," he said.

She recognized the melody then. It was "Forever."

"Will you dance with me?" he whispered, his eyes probing hers.

Kayla was too overcome with emotion to do anything but allow him to lead her onto the ice.

They began to glide with dreamy slowness in each other's arms. Their gazes locked as the blades of their skates cut watery paths in the ice. Their breaths mingled as one as their bodies drew closer together. In that moment when the music reached a crescendo, their lips met in a fiery kiss that told Kayla they had achieved perfect unison at last.

The music ended, but the dance wasn't over.

"Forever," Ryan told her. "That's how

long I want to hold you in my arms, Kayla. All night, every night, for as long as we both live."

She saw that his hands shook slightly as they framed her face, and her own lips trembled as she kissed his fingertips. "What are you saying, Ryan?"

He didn't answer for a moment. Releasing her, he stared into the darkness. "I've been into some pretty heavy denial, fighting my feelings for you, running scared."

She gently turned his face toward her. "Scared of me?"

"No." He drew his thumb across her cheek in a slow caress. "Just of royally ruining your plans for the future — your life — the way I always thought I'd ruined Gillian's. I cracked up my knee when I fell on an easy jump. It was a stupid accident that should never have happened."

"Accidents *do* happen, Ryan."

"I know." He gave a rueful laugh. "It's weird. At the time, I didn't think I'd done much harm. Maybe that's why I hovered over you when you twisted your ankle." His mouth hitched up on one side. "Too late I learned from the doc that my knee was a heck of a lot more damaged than I'd made myself believe. He gave me six years, you know." Ryan shook his head. "Gillian and I could have accomplished some great things in six years. But the knee wasn't all that I'd damaged."

Kayla's heart contracted in sympathy. "You mean your relationship with Gillian, don't you?"

His eyes reflected pain, but only for a moment. "I kept thinking if only I hadn't crossed that line, had kept our relationship on a professional level. As things worked out, she teamed with a guy who had about a tenth of her dedication and talent. And an insatiable craving for cocaine. Their partnership hit the skids. The guy went into rehab, and Gillian quit skating and went home to Cleveland, while I sat around nursing a wounded heart and a guilty conscience."

"I'm sorry."

"No, I've finally come to terms with it, laid the past to rest." Taking her hand, he placed a kiss in the palm. "A couple of days ago, Bill sent me a fax, an article about a new surgery that might buy me more time on the ice." He seemed to study her hand for a moment, as if it held some fascination for him. "Thing is, Kayla, I won't know until I see the doc. If he says it won't help, then —"

"Look at me," she interrupted. His head came up and he raised his eyes. Her lower lip quivered. "I love you, Ryan Maxwell!" she fairly shouted. Immediately, she sensed that the declaration had wrought a healing in her heart, her soul. "I *love* you," she said more softly. "Don't you see? It doesn't matter. We'll both coach at Bill's rink. That is, if he'll hire me."

"Hire you?" Ryan groaned. He pulled her into his arms and gazed down at her, hope shining in his eyes. "I'm crazy in love with you, Kayla," he said with a tenderness that stole her breath away.

They stood for a time without talking, content to hold each other close. Finally, Ryan drew back. A trace of apprehension clouded his eyes. "What about Brookings?"

"Hamil never met anything to me," she told him honestly. "I never signed a contract, though he offered me one. Once I told you that after my parents died, I began to pour all my energies and time into my career. It gave me a . . . reason for going on. A reason for living. The fact is I've been afraid of loving someone and losing them. I couldn't face the truth that I'd fallen in love with you because I was convinced we couldn't be together. But it happened," she said, smiling into his eyes, "and I can't fight it anymore."

"Don't fight it," he whispered, "because you're not going to lose me. Ever." His face relaxed in a grin. "What do you say we exchange these outfits for some genuine wedding duds?" His hold on her tightened. "Let's do it real soon."

"Is next week too soon? I've been wanting to go home for a visit. How does a winter wedding sound?"

"Wonderful. What do you say we honeymoon in Vienna after Worlds?"

She ran a finger lightly along his jaw. "I know the perfect place there," she said, shivering in anticipation at the vision of the two of them cocooned in the Tyrolean hotel.

As Ryan's mouth captured hers in a slow, sensuous kiss, Kayla knew that Meghan had been right. She wasn't forfeiting her dreams, only trading them in for one that was infinitely better.

About the Author

Marilyn Prather graduated from New Mexico University with a B.S. degree in elementary education. She enjoys writing poetry, as well as stories. She lives in Fort Myers, Florida, with her husband, David, and three cats.

The employees of Thorndike Press hope you have enjoyed this Large Print book. All our Thorndike and Wheeler Large Print titles are designed for easy reading, and all our books are made to last. Other Thorndike Press Large Print books are available at your library, through selected bookstores, or directly from us.

For information about titles, please call:

(800) 223-1244

or visit our Web site at:

www.gale.com/thorndike
www.gale.com/wheeler

To share your comments, please write:

Publisher
Thorndike Press
295 Kennedy Memorial Drive
Waterville, ME   04901